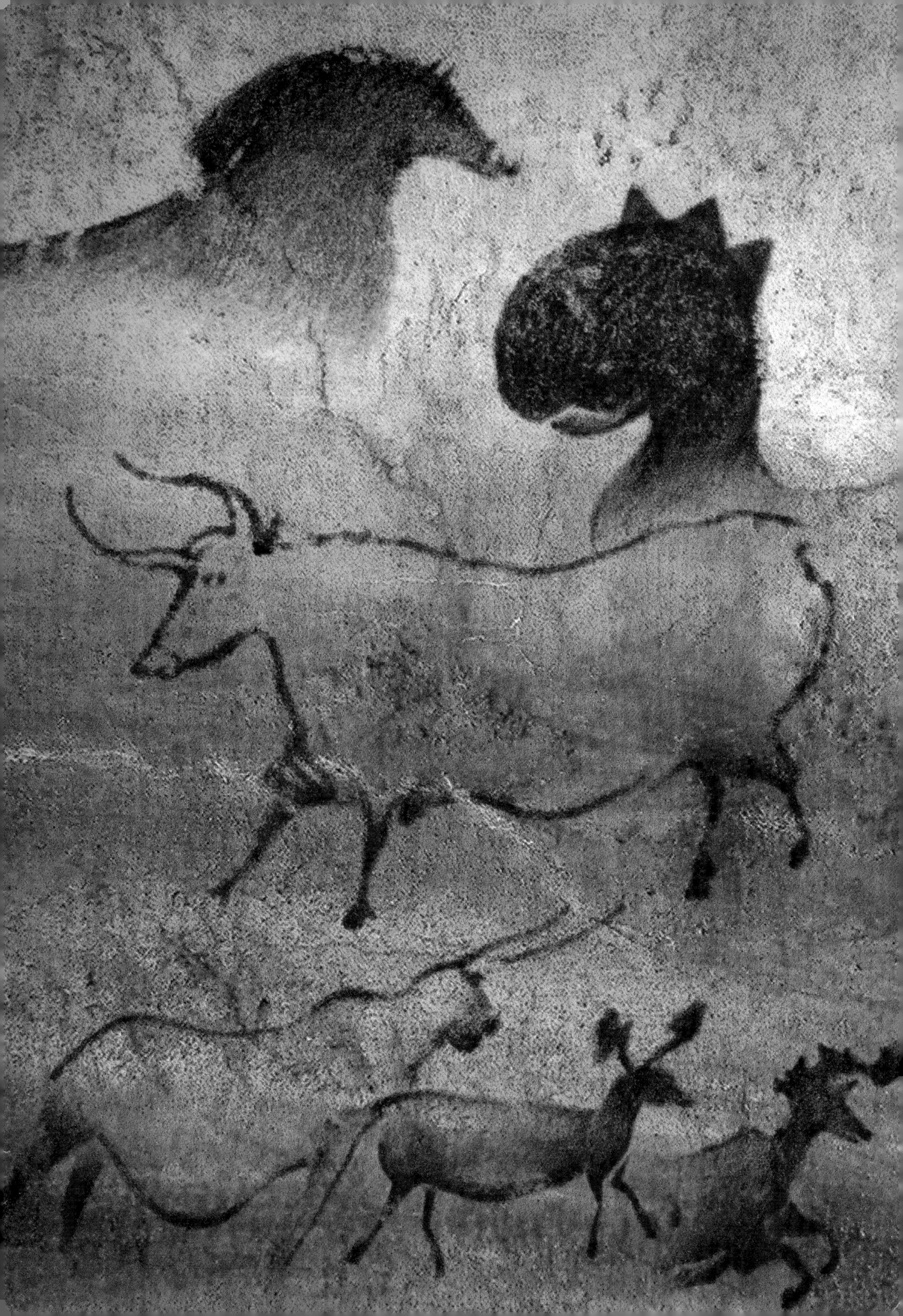

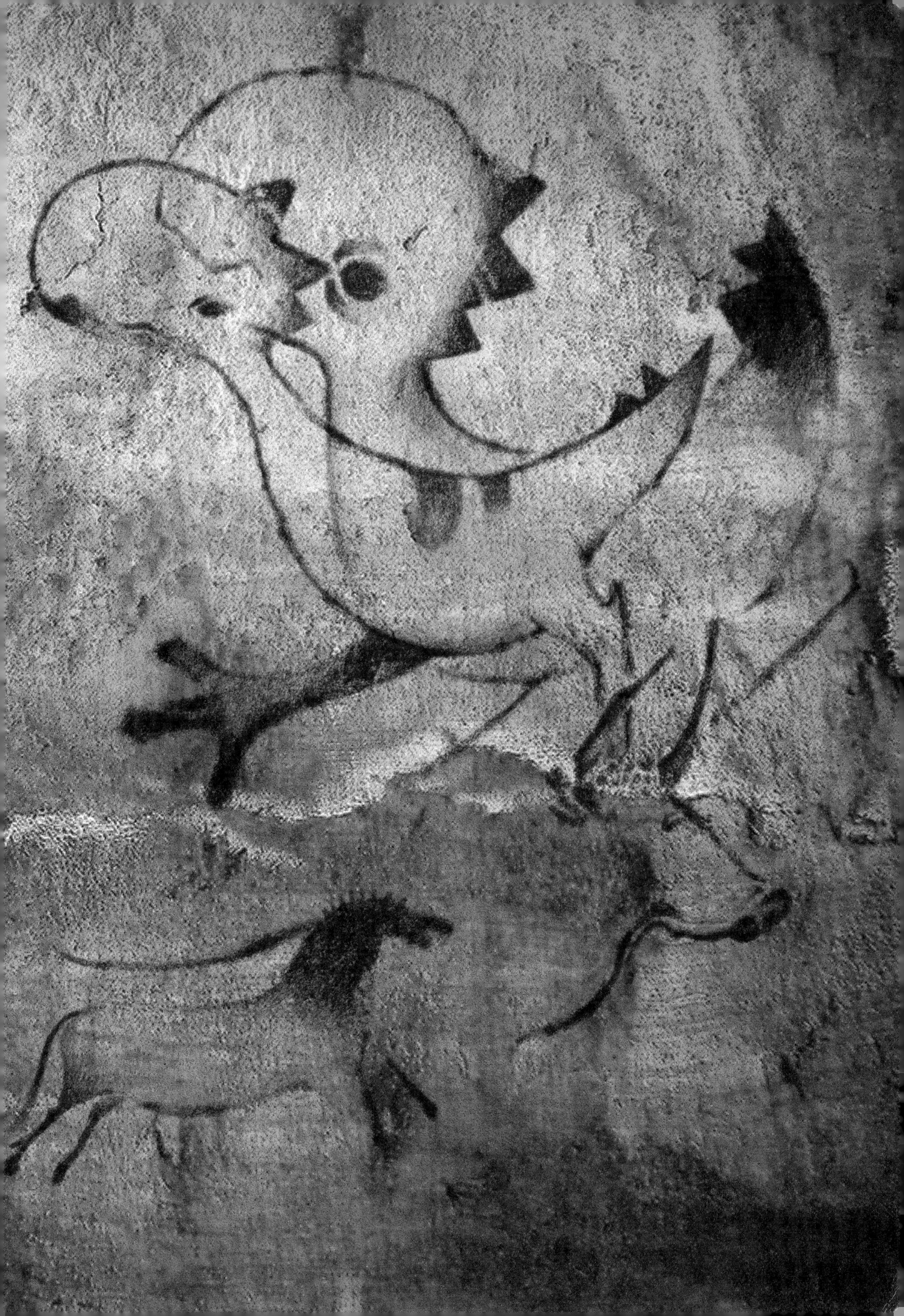

Tib & Tumtum #1

Welcome to the Tribe!

story
Grimaldi

art
Bannister

colors
Grimaldi

Graphic Universe™ • Minneapolis

To my mother Marie-Cécile, my grandmother Louise,
and my aunts Dominique and Catherine.
Thank you to my friends Elsa and Angélique, the queens of coloring.
And thanks to Fred for the Mac
--Grimaldi

Thank you to Christophe Bertschy and Fabien Vehlmann
--Bannister

Story by Grimaldi
Art by Bannister
Coloring by Grimaldi

Translation by Carol Klio Burrell

First American edition published in 2013 by Graphic Universe™.

Bienvenue au clan! by Grimaldi & Bannister © 2011—Glénat Editions
Copyright © 2013 by Lerner Publishing Group, Inc., for the US edition

Graphic Universe™ is a trademark of Lerner Publishing Group, Inc.

Graphic Universe™
A division of Lerner Publishing Group, Inc.
241 First Avenue North
Minneapolis, MN 55401 U.S.A.

Website address: www.lernerbooks.com

Library of Congress Cataloging-in-Publication Data

Grimaldi, 1975–
    [Bienvenue au clan! English.]
    Welcome to the tribe! / by Grimaldi ; illustrated by Bannister. — First American edition.
        p.   cm. — (Tib & Tumtum ; #1)
    Originally published in French in Grenoble, France, in 2011 by Glénat under the title: Bienvenue au clan!
    Summary: In a prehistoric era, Tib, a boy who is made fun of for his birthmark and his clumsiness,
 makes friends with Tumtum, a big, playful red dinosaur only he ever sees. When Tumtum saves the tribe's
 kids from a pack of hungry wolves, the shaman decides it's time to welcome a dinosaur into the tribe.
        ISBN 978-1-4677-1297-2 (lib. bdg. : alk. paper)
        ISBN 978-1-4677-1656-7 (eBook)
    1. Graphic novels. [1. Graphic novels. 2. Prehistoric peoples—Fiction. 3. Dinosaurs—Fiction.
    4. Birthmarks—Fiction.] I. Bannister, illustrator. II. Title.
    PZ7.7.6758We 2013
    741.5'944—dc23   2012047639

Manufactured in the United States of America
1 – BP – 7/15/13

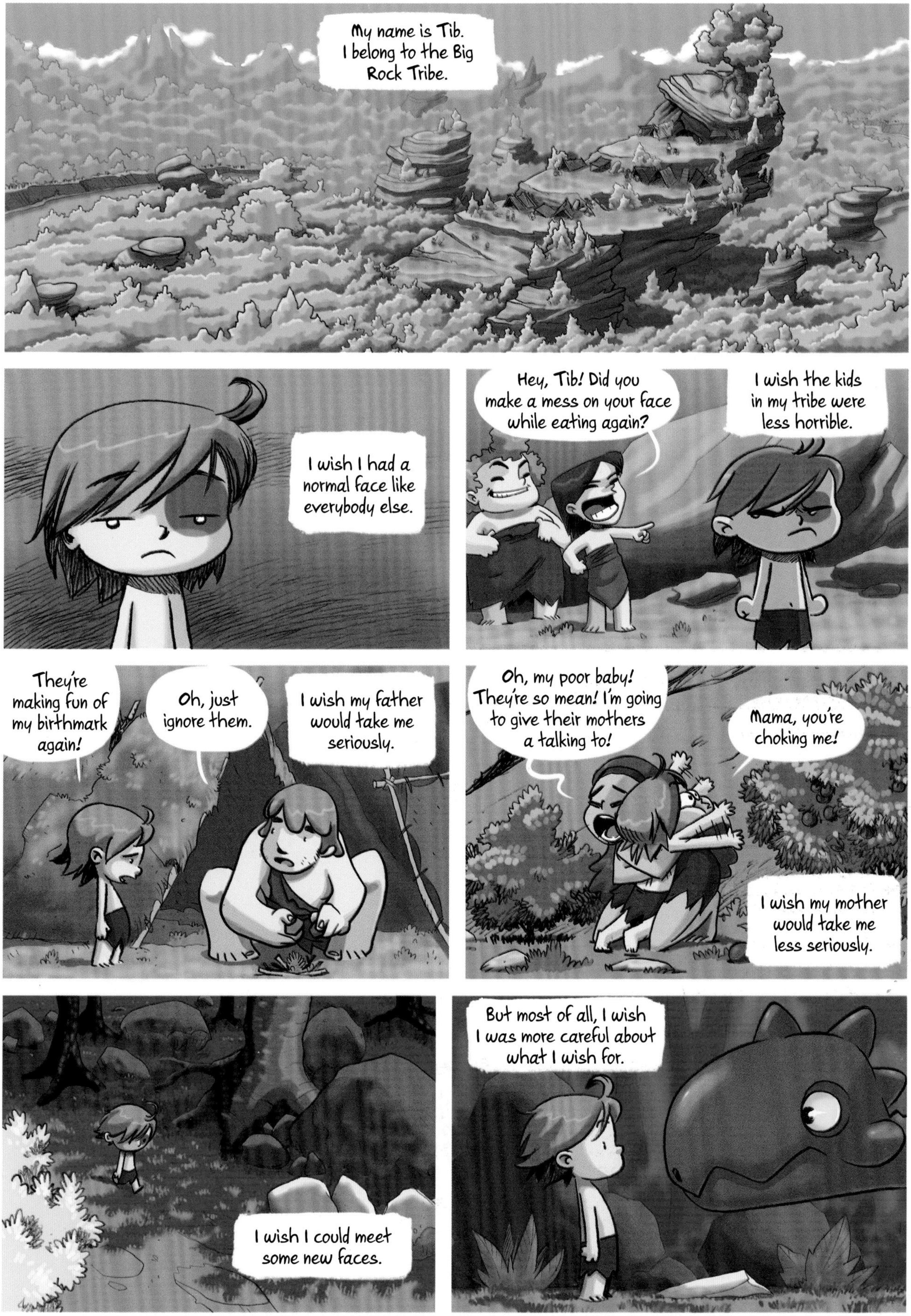
My name is Tib. I belong to the Big Rock Tribe.
I wish I had a normal face like everybody else.
Hey, Tib! Did you make a mess on your face while eating again?
I wish the kids in my tribe were less horrible.
They're making fun of my birthmark again!
Oh, just ignore them.
I wish my father would take me seriously.
Oh, my poor baby! They're so mean! I'm going to give their mothers a talking to!
Mama, you're choking me!
I wish my mother would take me less seriously.
I wish I could meet some new faces.
But most of all, I wish I was more careful about what I wish for.

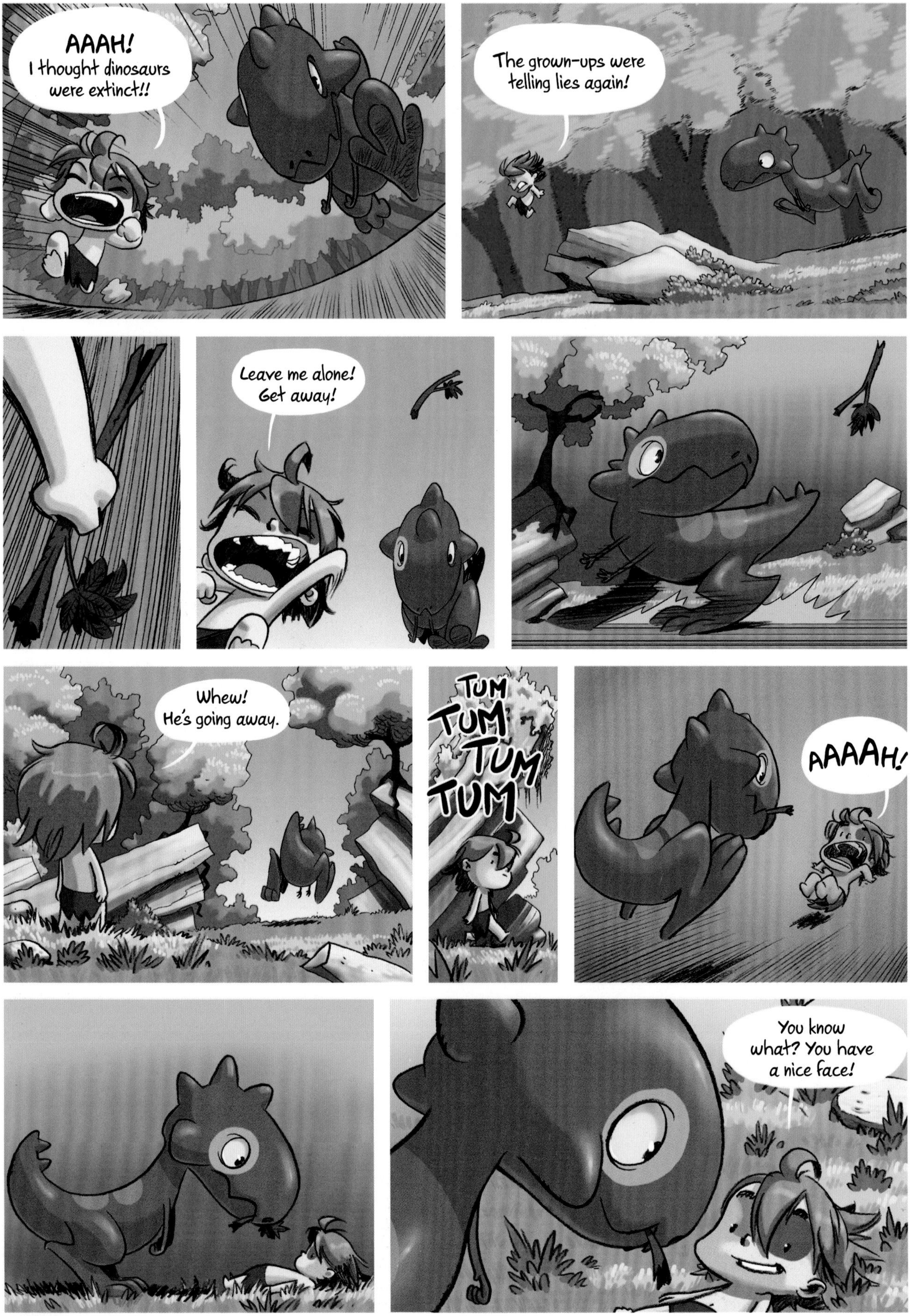
AAAH!
I thought dinosaurs were extinct!!
The grown-ups were telling lies again!
Leave me alone! Get away!
Whew! He's going away.
TUM TUM TUM TUM
AAAAH!
You know what? You have a nice face!

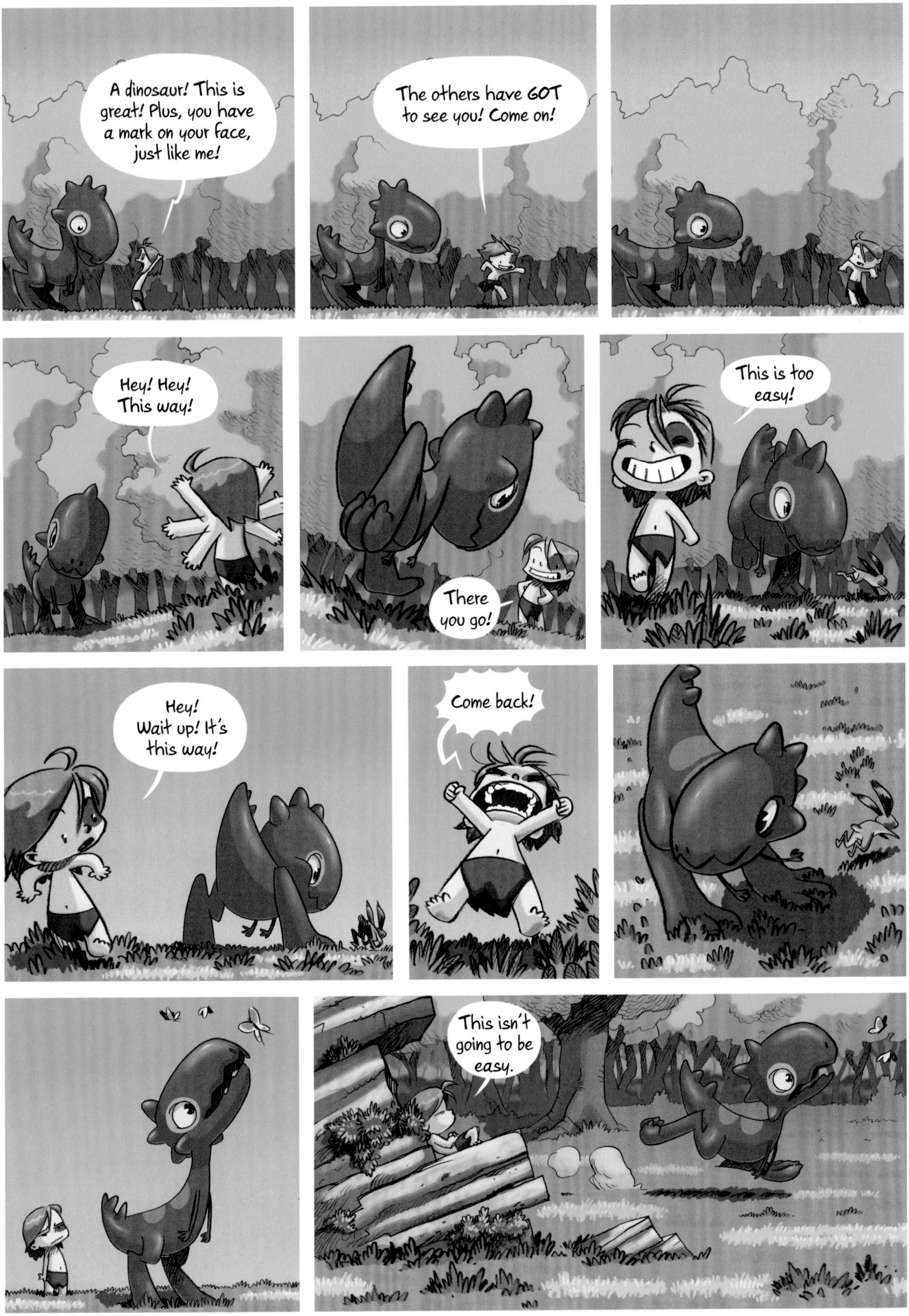
A dinosaur! This is great! Plus, you have a mark on your face, just like me!
The others have GOT to see you! Come on!
Hey! Hey! This way!
There you go!
This is too easy!
Hey! Wait up! It's this way!
Come back!
This isn't going to be easy.

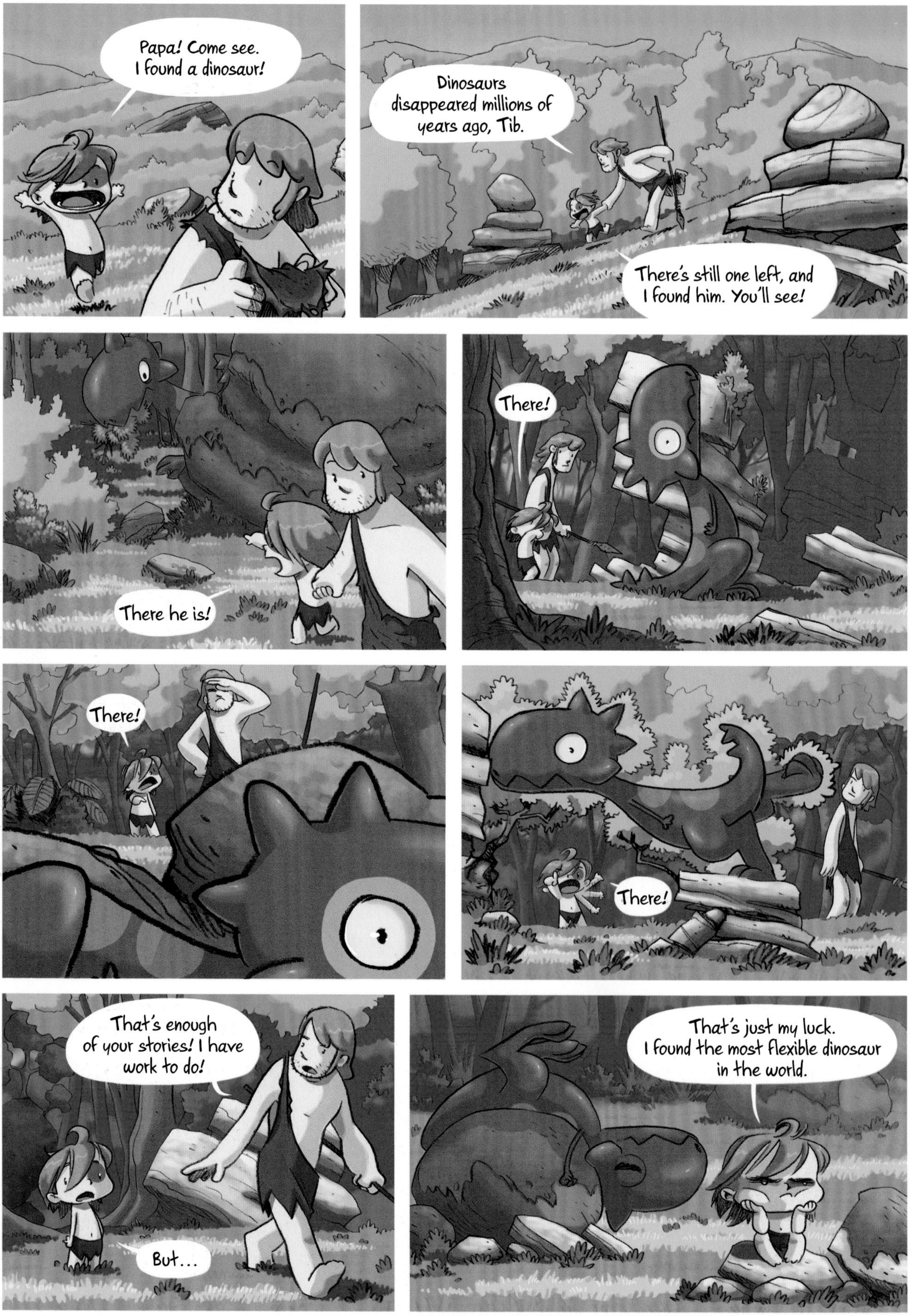

Papa! Come see. I found a dinosaur!
Dinosaurs disappeared millions of years ago, Tib.
There's still one left, and I found him. You'll see!
There he is!
There!
There!
There!
That's enough of your stories! I have work to do!
But...
That's just my luck. I found the most flexible dinosaur in the world.

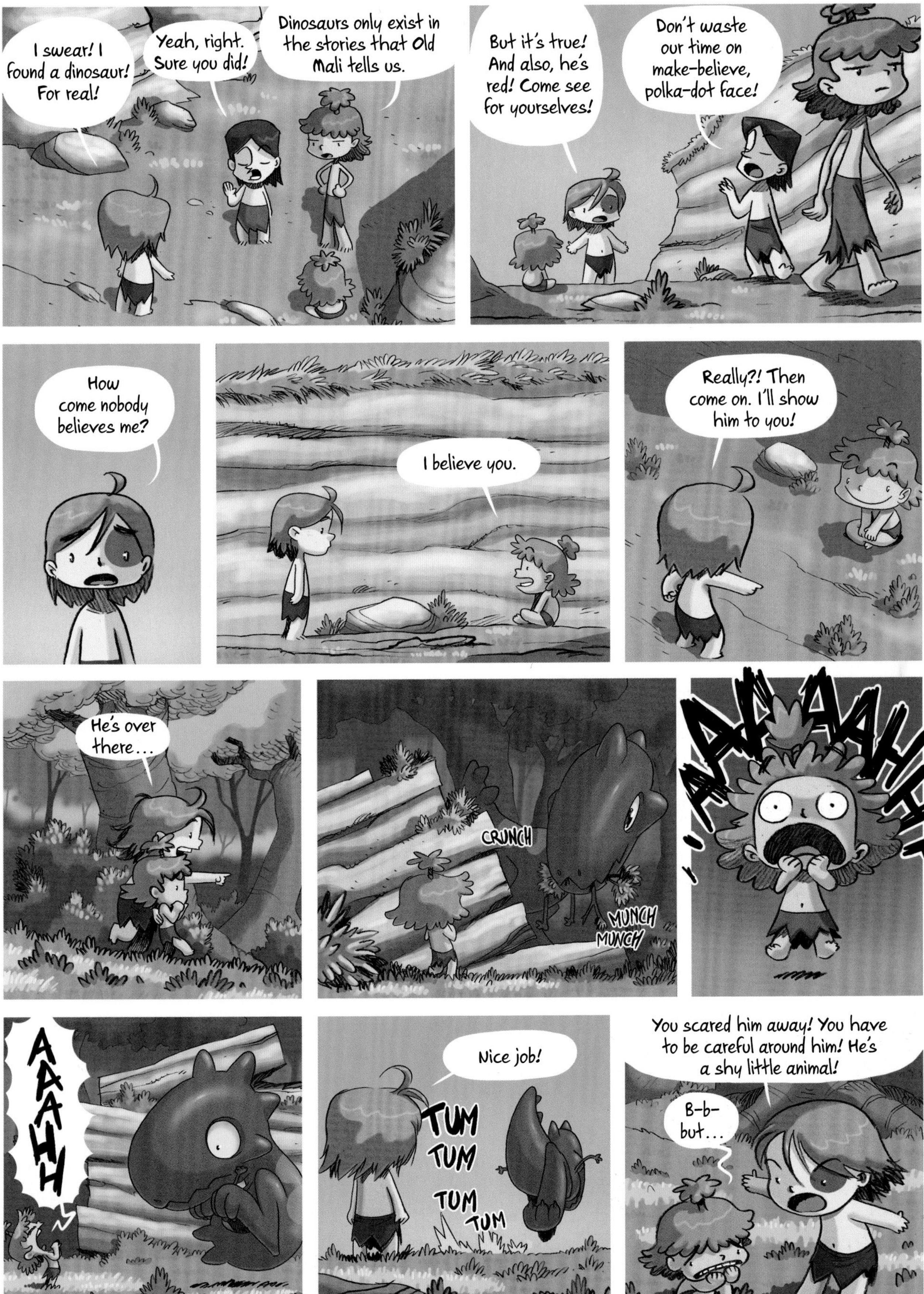
I swear! I found a dinosaur! For real!
Yeah, right. Sure you did!
Dinosaurs only exist in the stories that Old Mali tells us.
But it's true! And also, he's red! Come see for yourselves!
Don't waste our time on make-believe, polka-dot face!
How come nobody believes me?
I believe you.
Really?! Then come on. I'll show him to you!
He's over there…
CRUNCH
MUNCH MUNCH
AAAAAHH!
AAAHH
Nice job!
TUM TUM TUM TUM
You scared him away! You have to be careful around him! He's a shy little animal!
B-b-but…

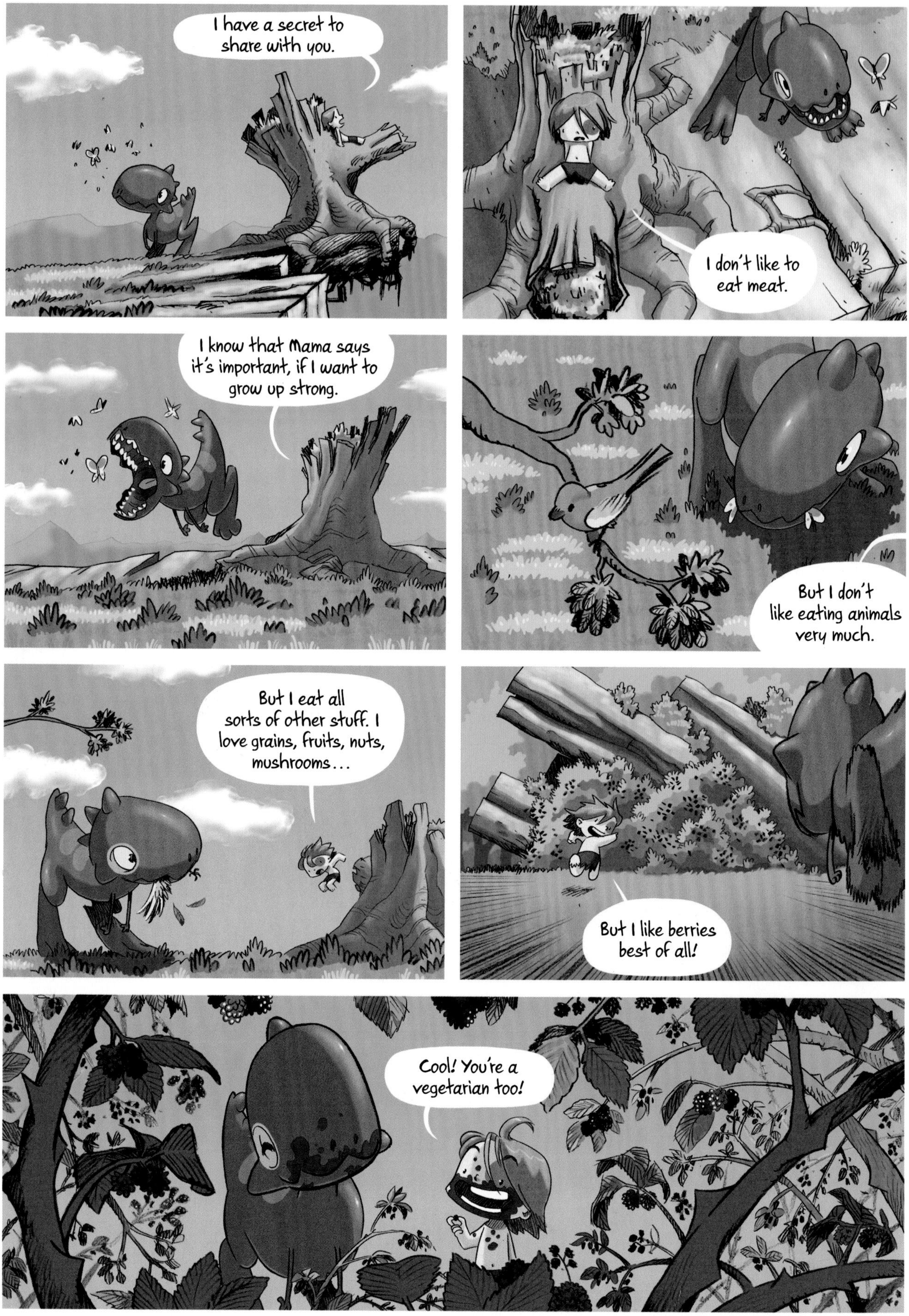
I have a secret to share with you.
I don't like to eat meat.
I know that Mama says it's important, if I want to grow up strong.
But I don't like eating animals very much.
But I eat all sorts of other stuff. I love grains, fruits, nuts, mushrooms...
But I like berries best of all!
Cool! You're a vegetarian too!

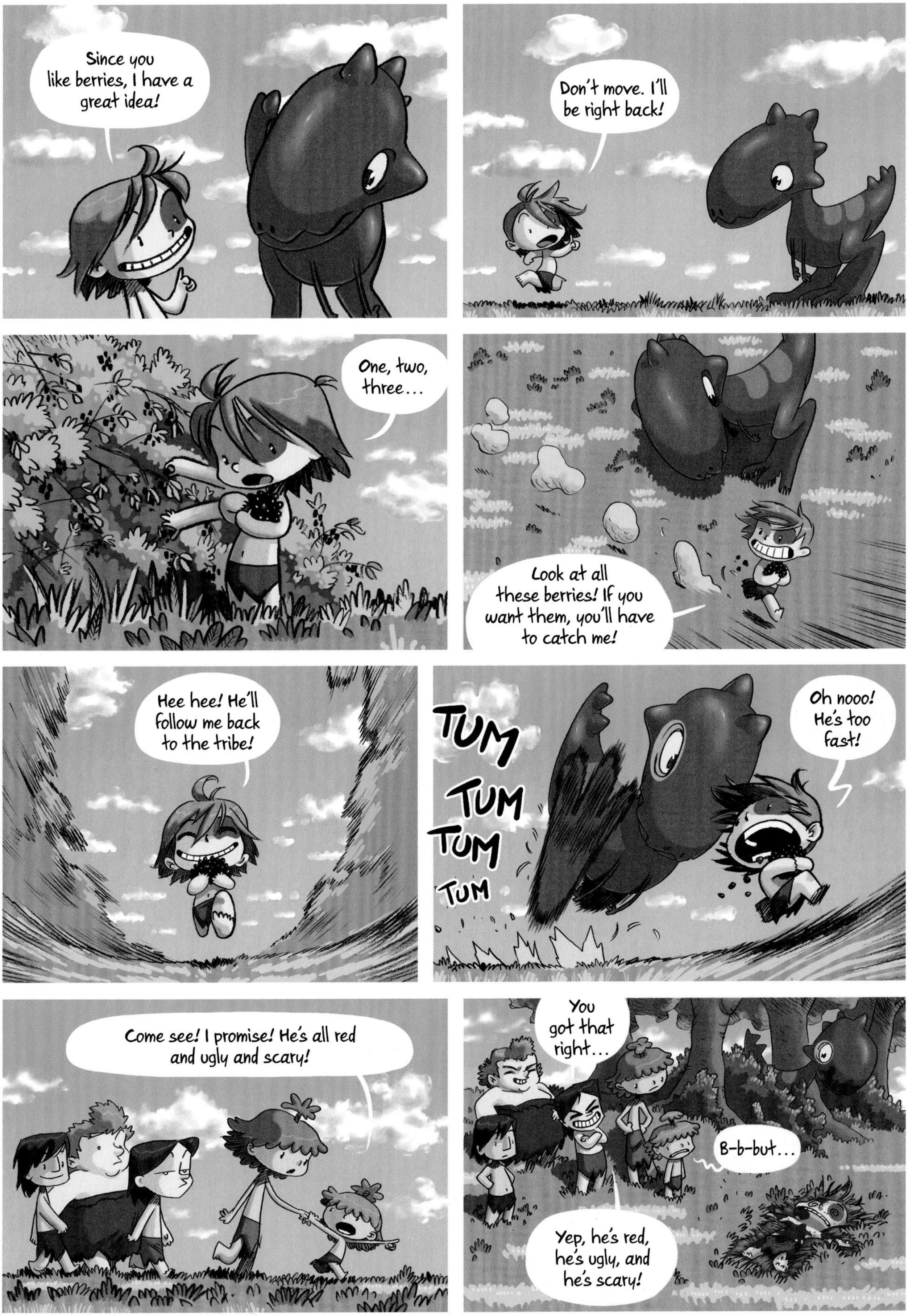
Since you like berries, I have a great idea!
Don't move. I'll be right back!
One, two, three...
Look at all these berries! If you want them, you'll have to catch me!
Hee hee! He'll follow me back to the tribe!
TUM
TUM
TUM
TUM
Oh nooo! He's too fast!
Come see! I promise! He's all red and ugly and scary!
You got that right...
B-b-but...
Yep, he's red, he's ugly, and he's scary!

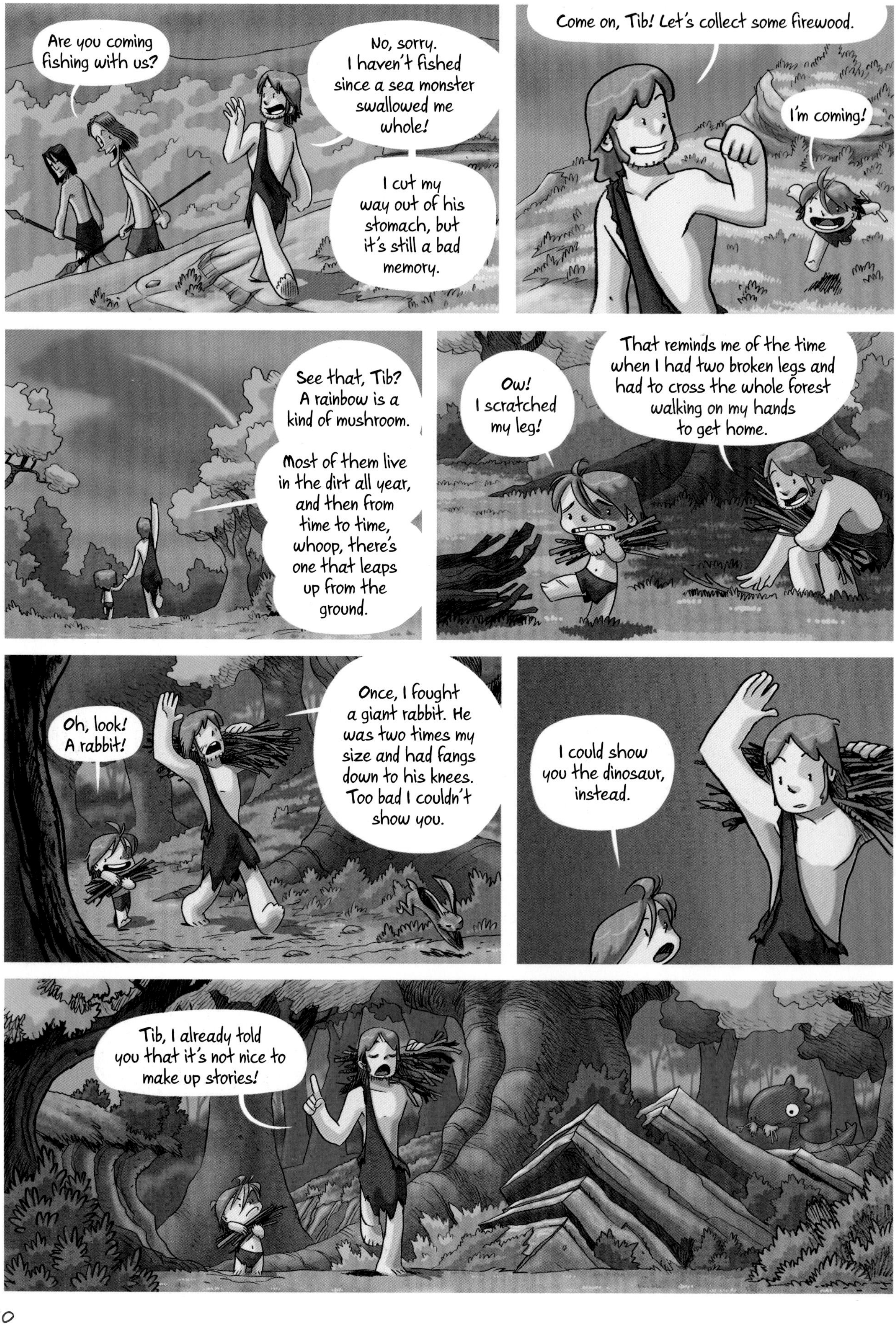
Are you coming fishing with us?
No, sorry. I haven't fished since a sea monster swallowed me whole!
I cut my way out of his stomach, but it's still a bad memory.
Come on, Tib! Let's collect some firewood.
I'm coming!
See that, Tib? A rainbow is a kind of mushroom.
Most of them live in the dirt all year, and then from time to time, whoop, there's one that leaps up from the ground.
Ow! I scratched my leg!
That reminds me of the time when I had two broken legs and had to cross the whole forest walking on my hands to get home.
Oh, look! A rabbit!
Once, I fought a giant rabbit. He was two times my size and had fangs down to his knees. Too bad I couldn't show you.
I could show you the dinosaur, instead.
Tib, I already told you that it's not nice to make up stories!

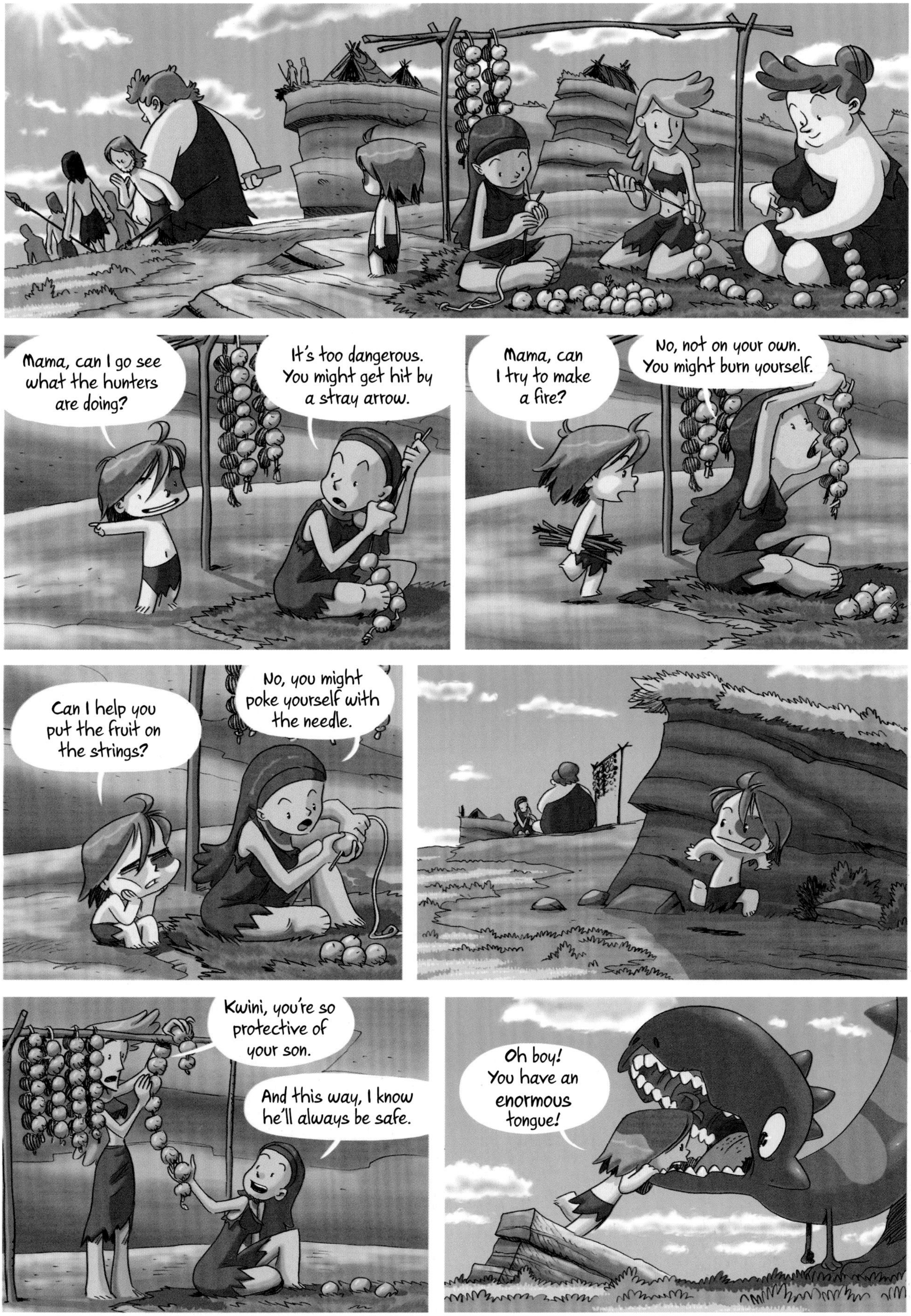
Mama, can I go see what the hunters are doing?
It's too dangerous. You might get hit by a stray arrow.
Mama, can I try to make a fire?
No, not on your own. You might burn yourself.
Can I help you put the fruit on the strings?
No, you might poke yourself with the needle.
Kwini, you're so protective of your son.
And this way, I know he'll always be safe.
Oh boy! You have an enormous tongue!

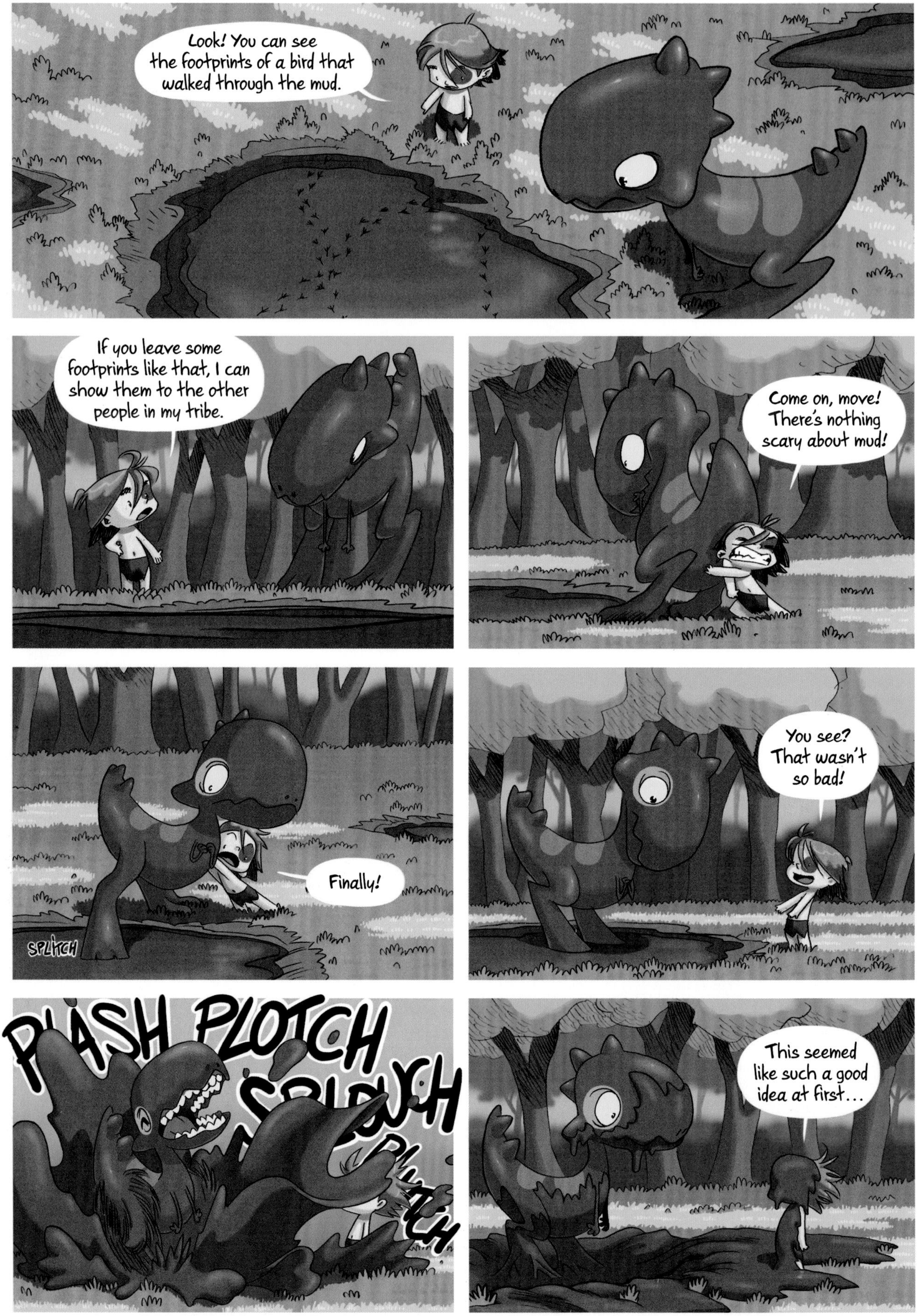
Look! You can see the footprints of a bird that walked through the mud.
If you leave some footprints like that, I can show them to the other people in my tribe.
Come on, move! There's nothing scary about mud!
SPLITCH
Finally!
You see? That wasn't so bad!
PLASH PLOTCH
This seemed like such a good idea at first…

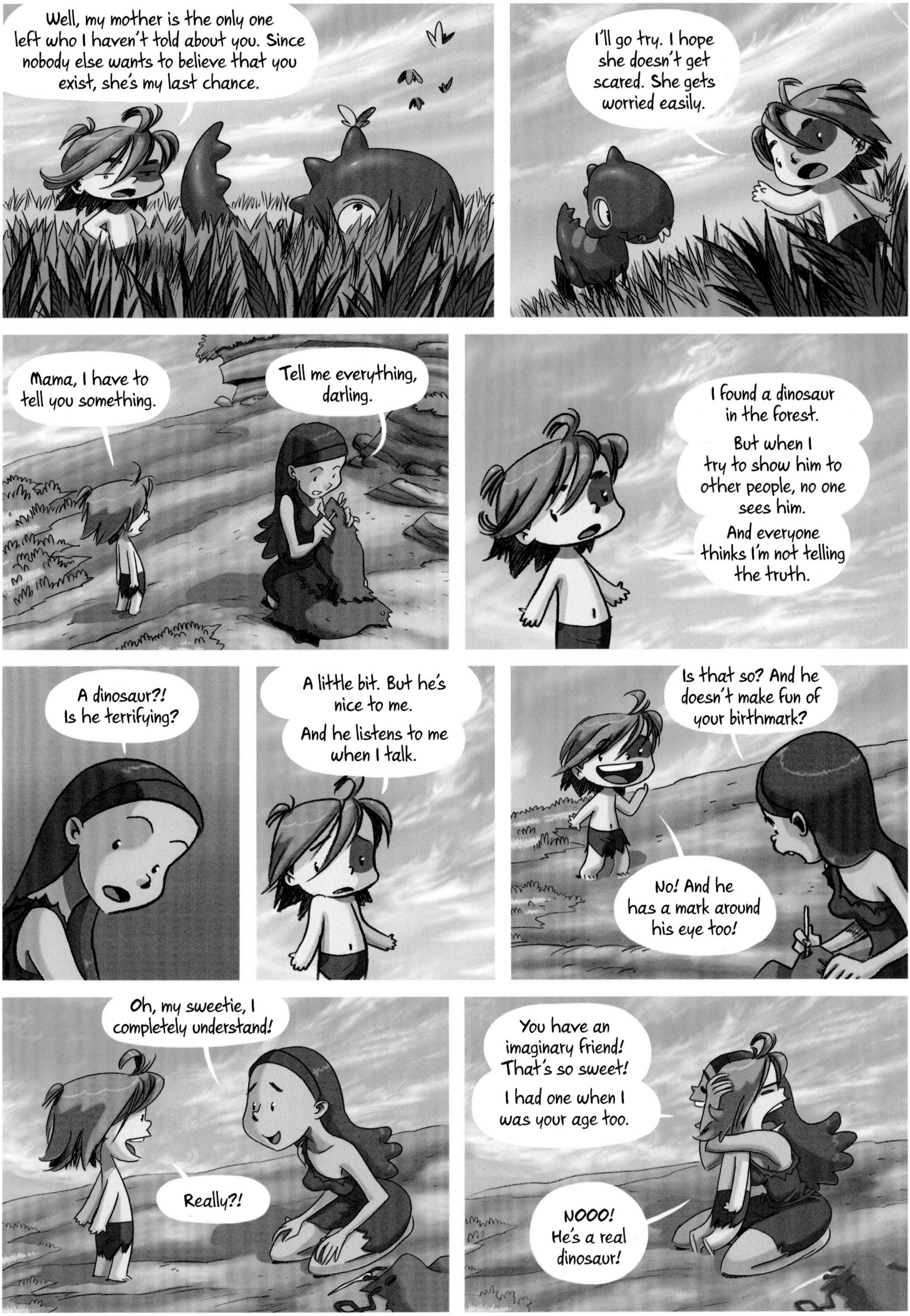

Well, my mother is the only one left who I haven't told about you. Since nobody else wants to believe that you exist, she's my last chance.
I'll go try. I hope she doesn't get scared. She gets worried easily.
Mama, I have to tell you something.
Tell me everything, darling.
I found a dinosaur in the forest.
But when I try to show him to other people, no one sees him.
And everyone thinks I'm not telling the truth.
A dinosaur?! Is he terrifying?
A little bit. But he's nice to me.
And he listens to me when I talk.
Is that so? And he doesn't make fun of your birthmark?
No! And he has a mark around his eye too!
Oh, my sweetie, I completely understand!
Really?!
You have an imaginary friend! That's so sweet!
I had one when I was your age too.
NOOO! He's a real dinosaur!

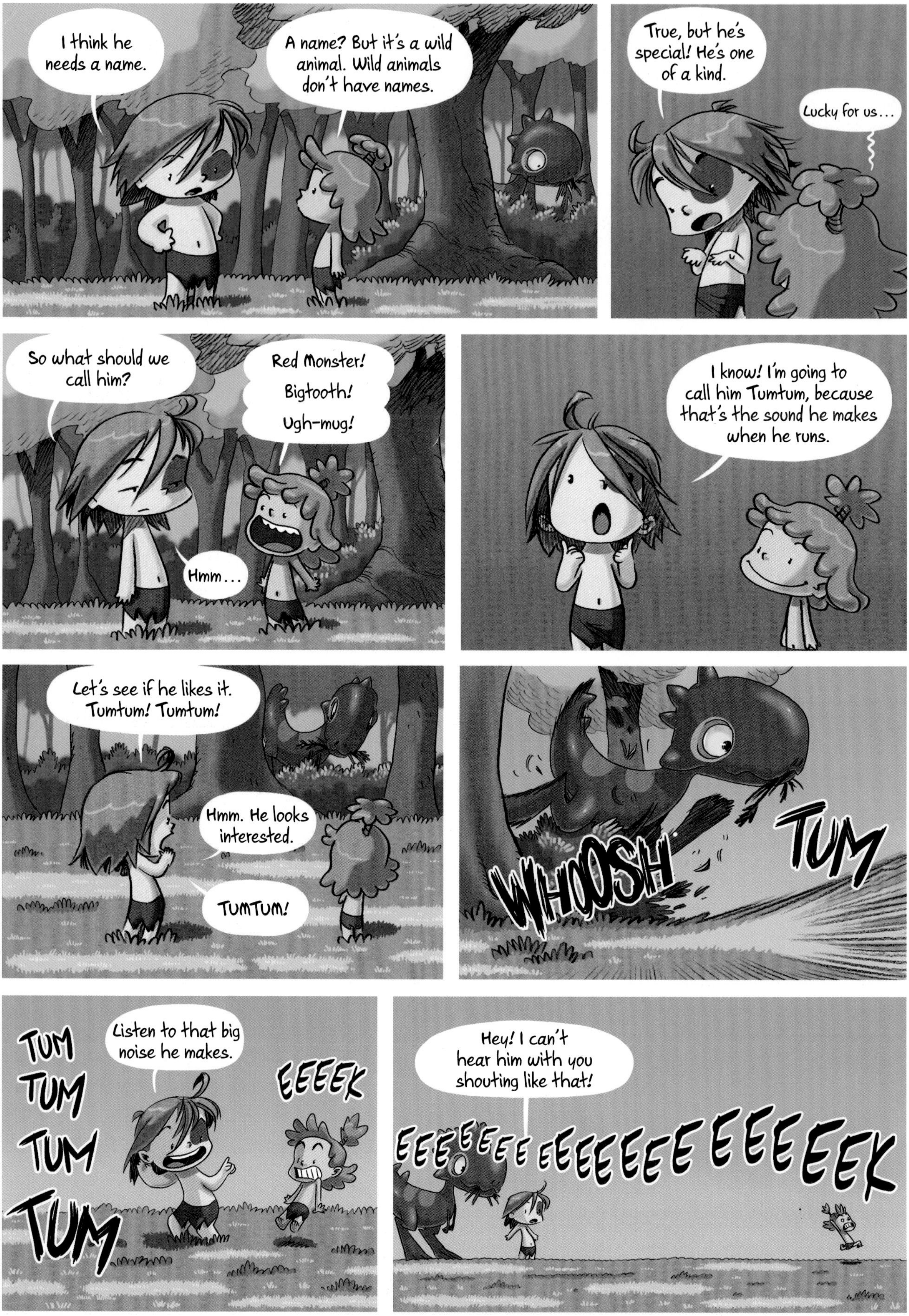
I think he needs a name.
A name? But it's a wild animal. Wild animals don't have names.
True, but he's special! He's one of a kind.
Lucky for us...
So what should we call him?
Red Monster! Bigtooth! Ugh-mug!
Hmm...
I know! I'm going to call him Tumtum, because that's the sound he makes when he runs.
Let's see if he likes it. Tumtum! Tumtum!
Hmm. He looks interested.
TUMTUM!
WHOOSH
TUM
TUM TUM TUM TUM
Listen to that big noise he makes.
EEEEK
Hey! I can't hear him with you shouting like that!
EEEEEEEEEEEEEEEEEEEEEK

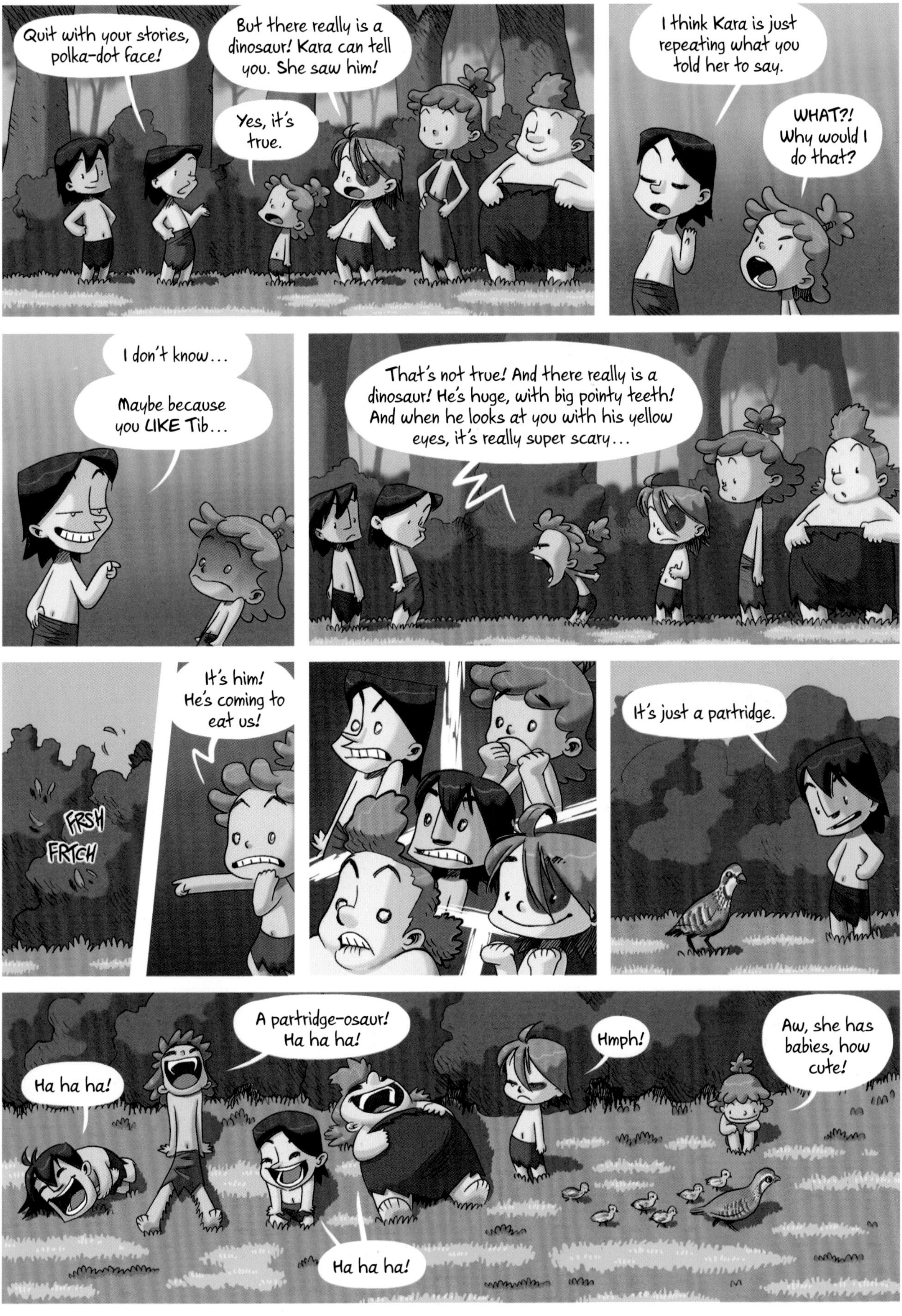
Quit with your stories, polka-dot face!
But there really is a dinosaur! Kara can tell you. She saw him!
Yes, it's true.
I think Kara is just repeating what you told her to say.
WHAT?! Why would I do that?
I don't know...
Maybe because you LIKE Tib...
That's not true! And there really is a dinosaur! He's huge, with big pointy teeth! And when he looks at you with his yellow eyes, it's really super scary...
FRSH
FRTCH
It's him! He's coming to eat us!
It's just a partridge.
Ha ha ha!
A partridge-osaur! Ha ha ha!
Hmph!
Aw, she has babies, how cute!
Ha ha ha!

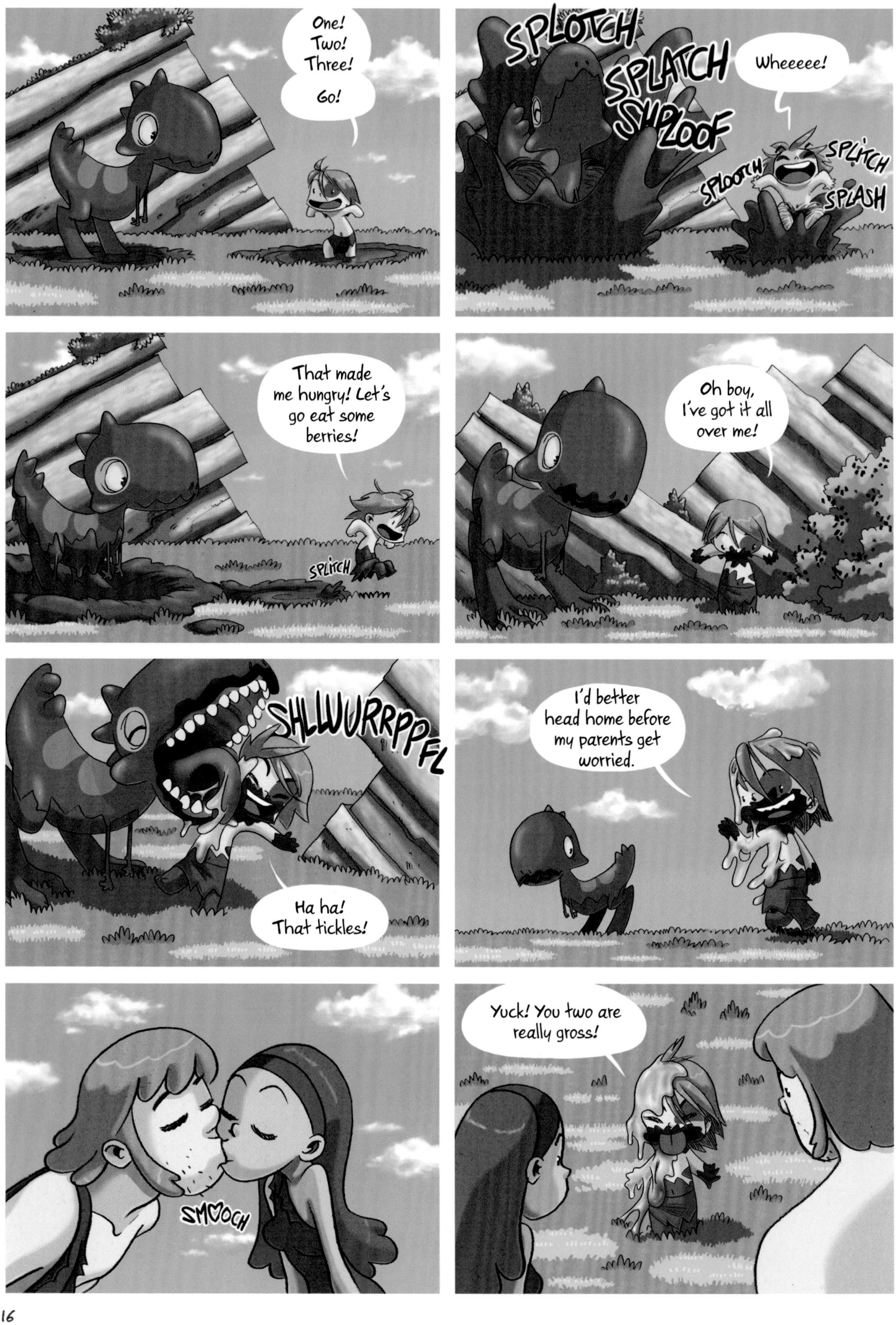
One! Two! Three!
Go!
SPLOTCH
SPLATCH
SHPLOOF
Wheeeee!
SPLOOTCH
SPLITCH
SPLASH
That made me hungry! Let's go eat some berries!
SPLITCH
Oh boy, I've got it all over me!
SHLWURRPPFL
Ha ha! That tickles!
I'd better head home before my parents get worried.
SMOOCH
Yuck! You two are really gross!

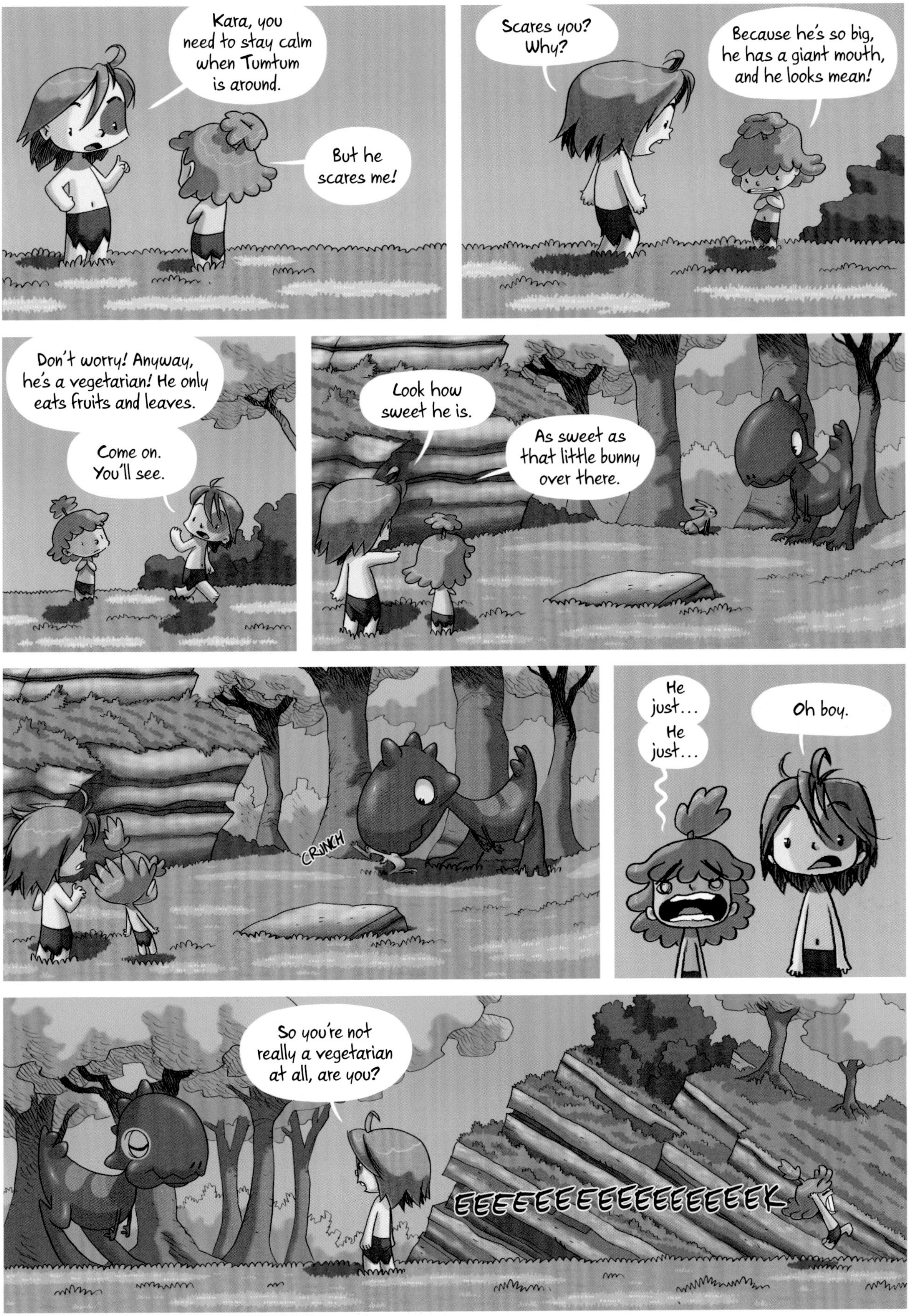
Kara, you need to stay calm when Tumtum is around.
But he scares me!
Scares you? Why?
Because he's so big, he has a giant mouth, and he looks mean!
Don't worry! Anyway, he's a vegetarian! He only eats fruits and leaves.
Come on. You'll see.
Look how sweet he is.
As sweet as that little bunny over there.
CRUNCH
He just...
He just...
Oh boy.
So you're not really a vegetarian at all, are you?
EEEEEEEEEEEEEEEEEK

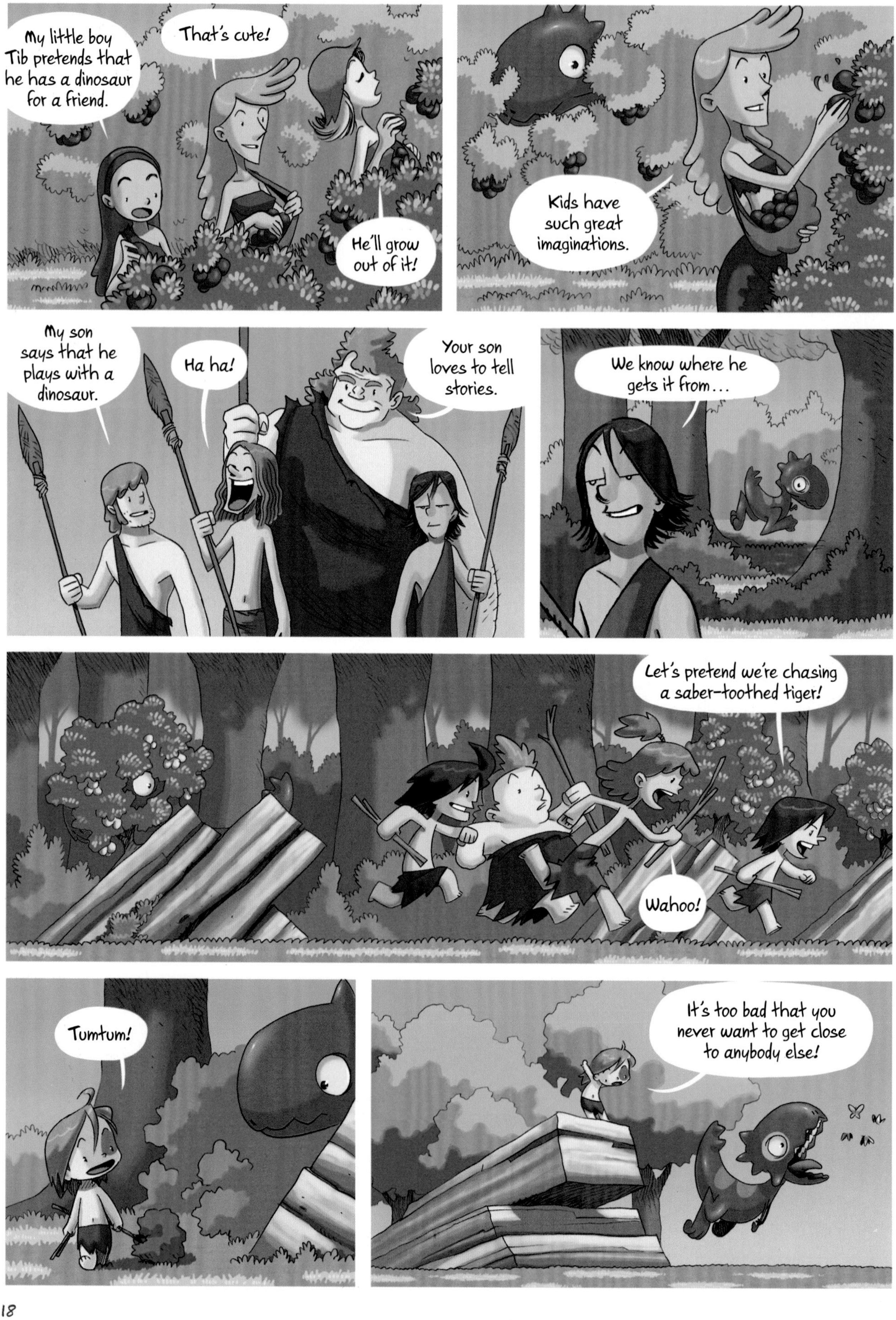
My little boy Tib pretends that he has a dinosaur for a friend.
That's cute!
He'll grow out of it!
Kids have such great imaginations.
My son says that he plays with a dinosaur.
Ha ha!
Your son loves to tell stories.
We know where he gets it from...
Let's pretend we're chasing a saber-toothed tiger!
Wahoo!
Tumtum!
It's too bad that you never want to get close to anybody else!

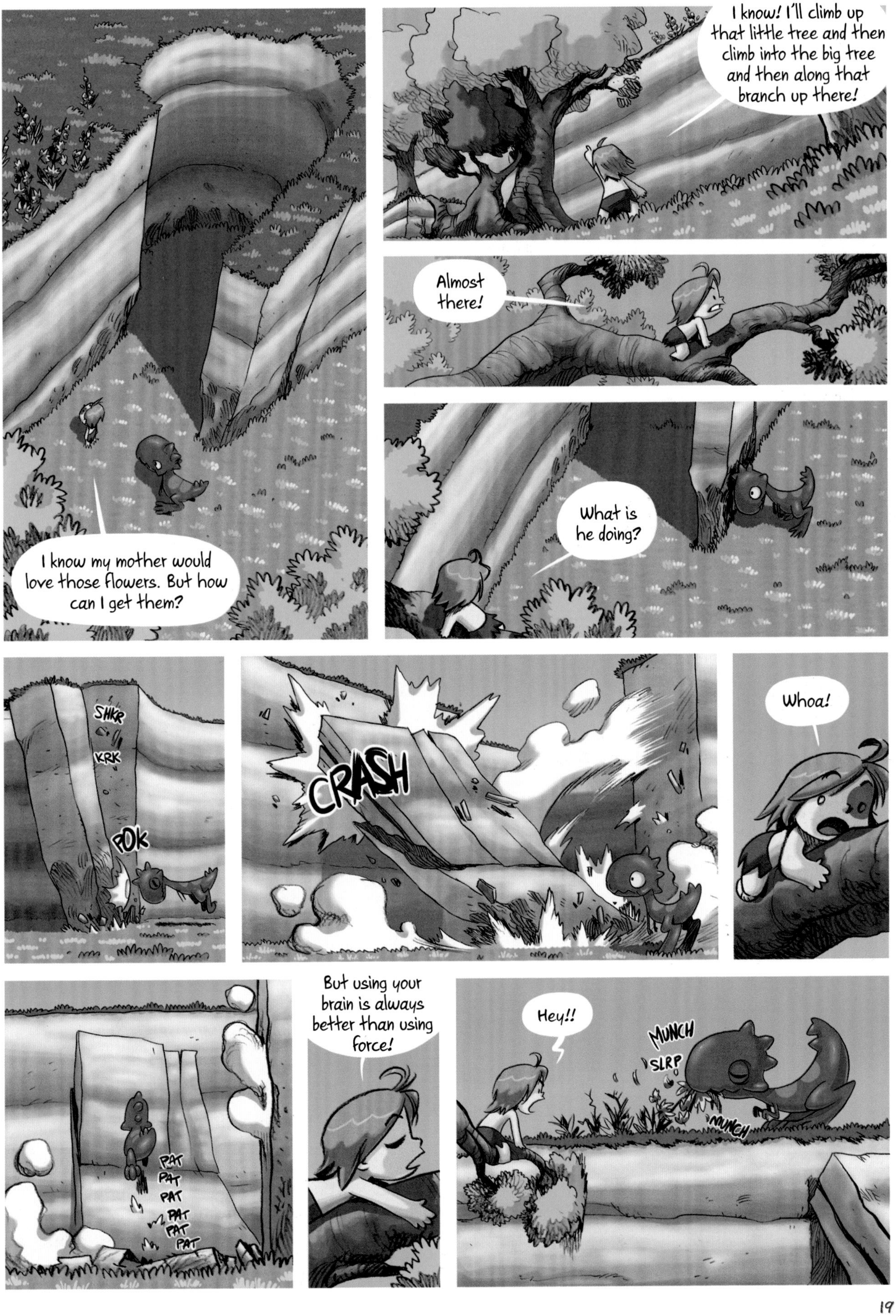
I know my mother would love those flowers. But how can I get them?
I know! I'll climb up that little tree and then climb into the big tree and then along that branch up there!
Almost there!
What is he doing?
SHKR
KRK
POK
CRASH
Whoa!
PAT PAT PAT PAT PAT PAT
But using your brain is always better than using force!
Hey!!
MUNCH
SLRP
MUNCH

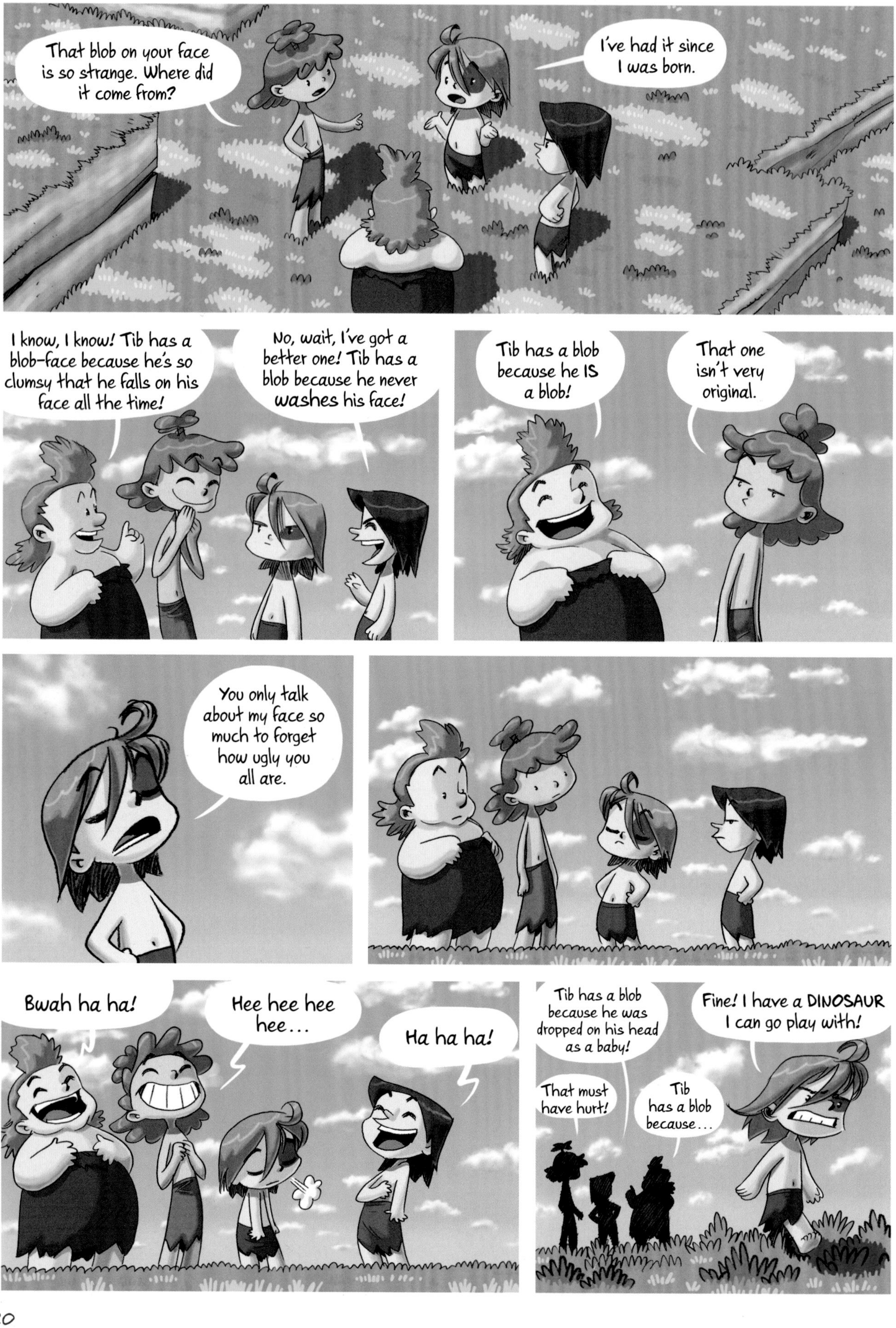

That blob on your face is so strange. Where did it come from?
I've had it since I was born.
I know, I know! Tib has a blob-face because he's so clumsy that he falls on his face all the time!
No, wait, I've got a better one! Tib has a blob because he never washes his face!
Tib has a blob because he IS a blob!
That one isn't very original.
You only talk about my face so much to forget how ugly you all are.
Bwah ha ha!
Hee hee hee hee...
Ha ha ha!
Tib has a blob because he was dropped on his head as a baby!
That must have hurt!
Tib has a blob because...
Fine! I have a DINOSAUR I can go play with!

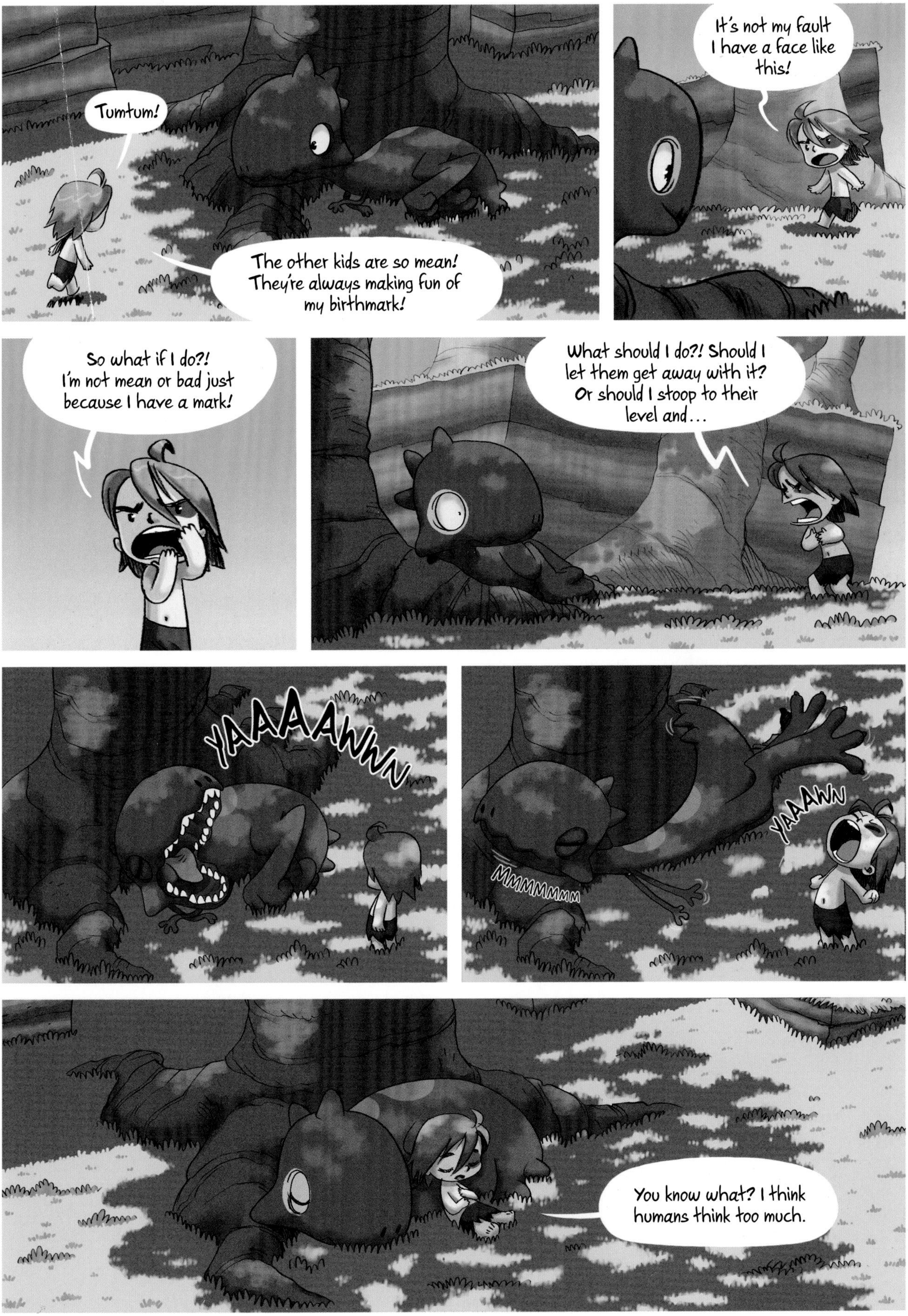
Tumtum!
The other kids are so mean! They're always making fun of my birthmark!
It's not my fault I have a face like this!
So what if I do?! I'm not mean or bad just because I have a mark!
What should I do?! Should I let them get away with it? Or should I stoop to their level and...
YAAAAAWWN
MMMMMMMM
YAAAWN
You know what? I think humans think too much.

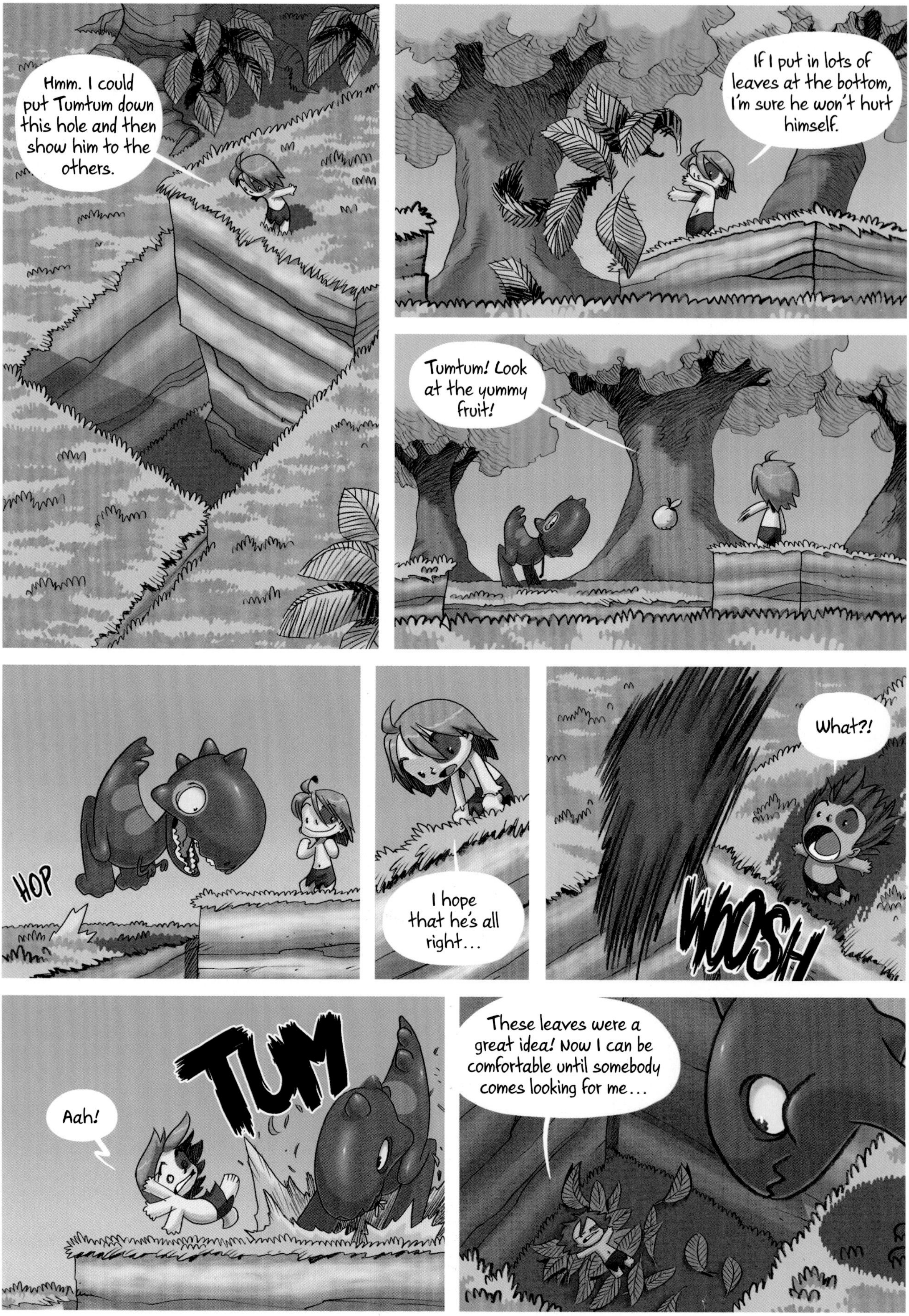

Hmm. I could put Tumtum down this hole and then show him to the others.
If I put in lots of leaves at the bottom, I'm sure he won't hurt himself.
Tumtum! Look at the yummy fruit!
HOP
I hope that he's all right...
What?!
WOOSH
Aah!
TUM
These leaves were a great idea! Now I can be comfortable until somebody comes looking for me...

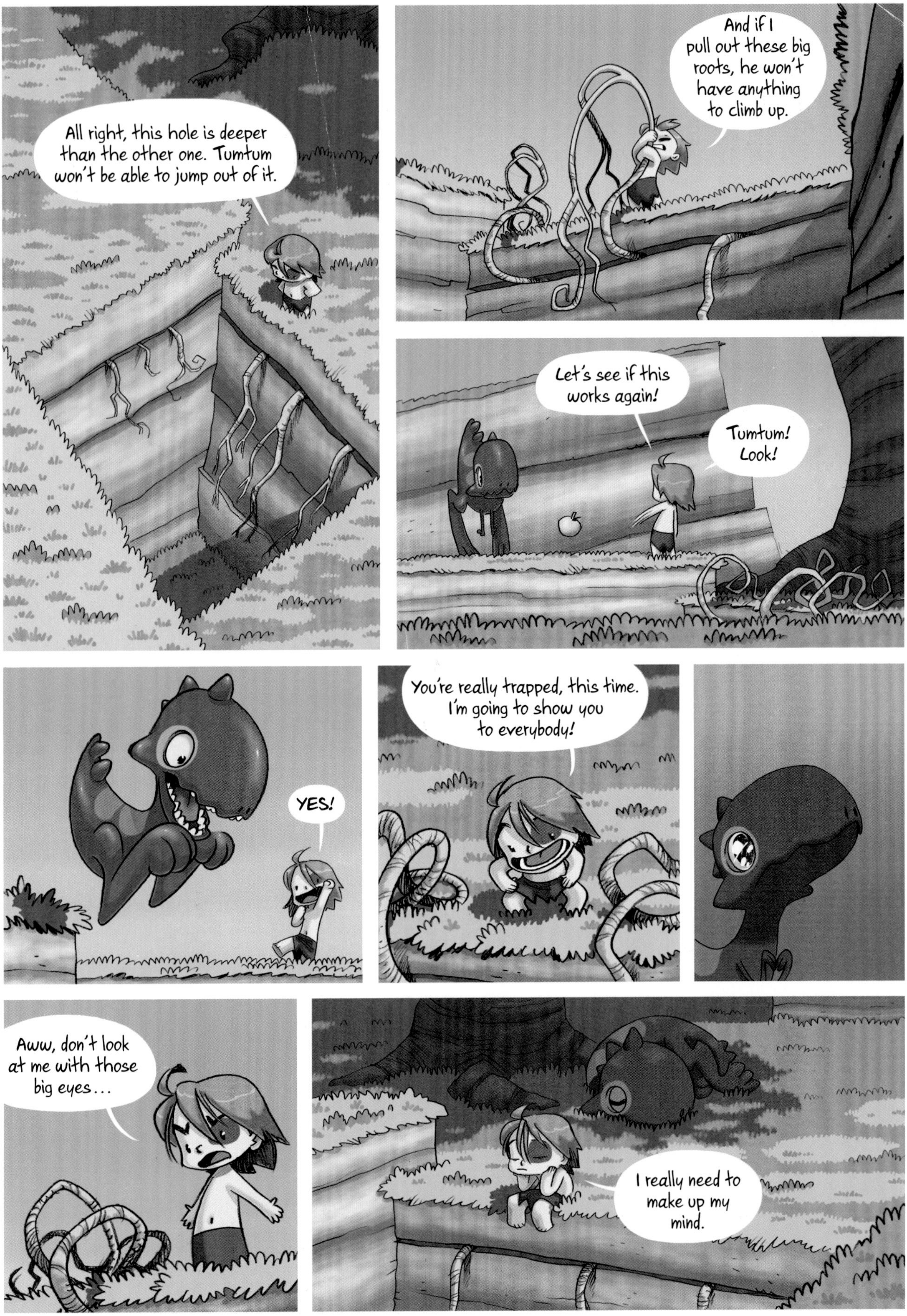
All right, this hole is deeper than the other one. Tumtum won't be able to jump out of it.
And if I pull out these big roots, he won't have anything to climb up.
Let's see if this works again!
Tumtum! Look!
YES!
You're really trapped, this time. I'm going to show you to everybody!
Aww, don't look at me with those big eyes...
I really need to make up my mind.

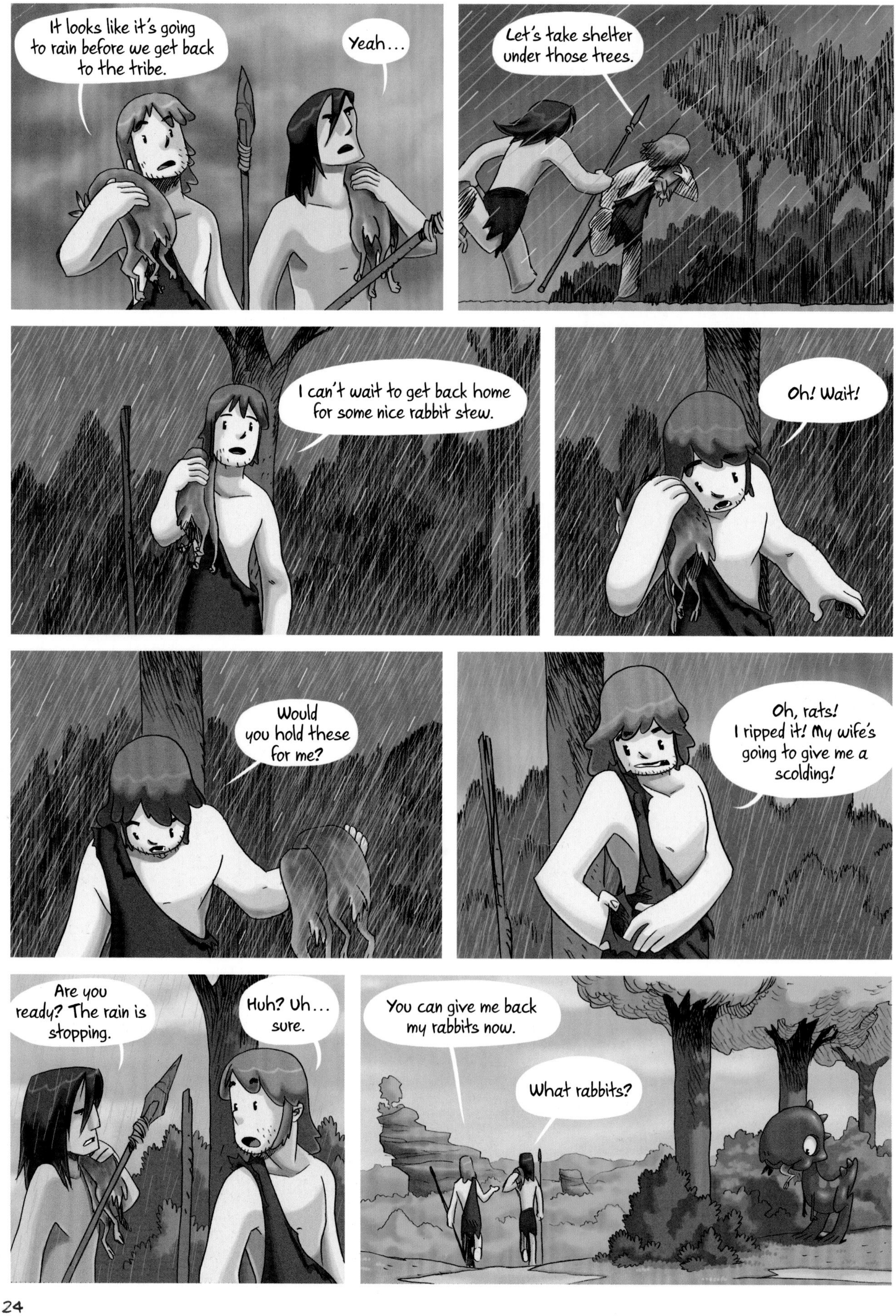
It looks like it's going to rain before we get back to the tribe.
Yeah...
Let's take shelter under those trees.
I can't wait to get back home for some nice rabbit stew.
Oh! Wait!
Would you hold these for me?
Oh, rats! I ripped it! My wife's going to give me a scolding!
Are you ready? The rain is stopping.
Huh? Uh... sure.
You can give me back my rabbits now.
What rabbits?

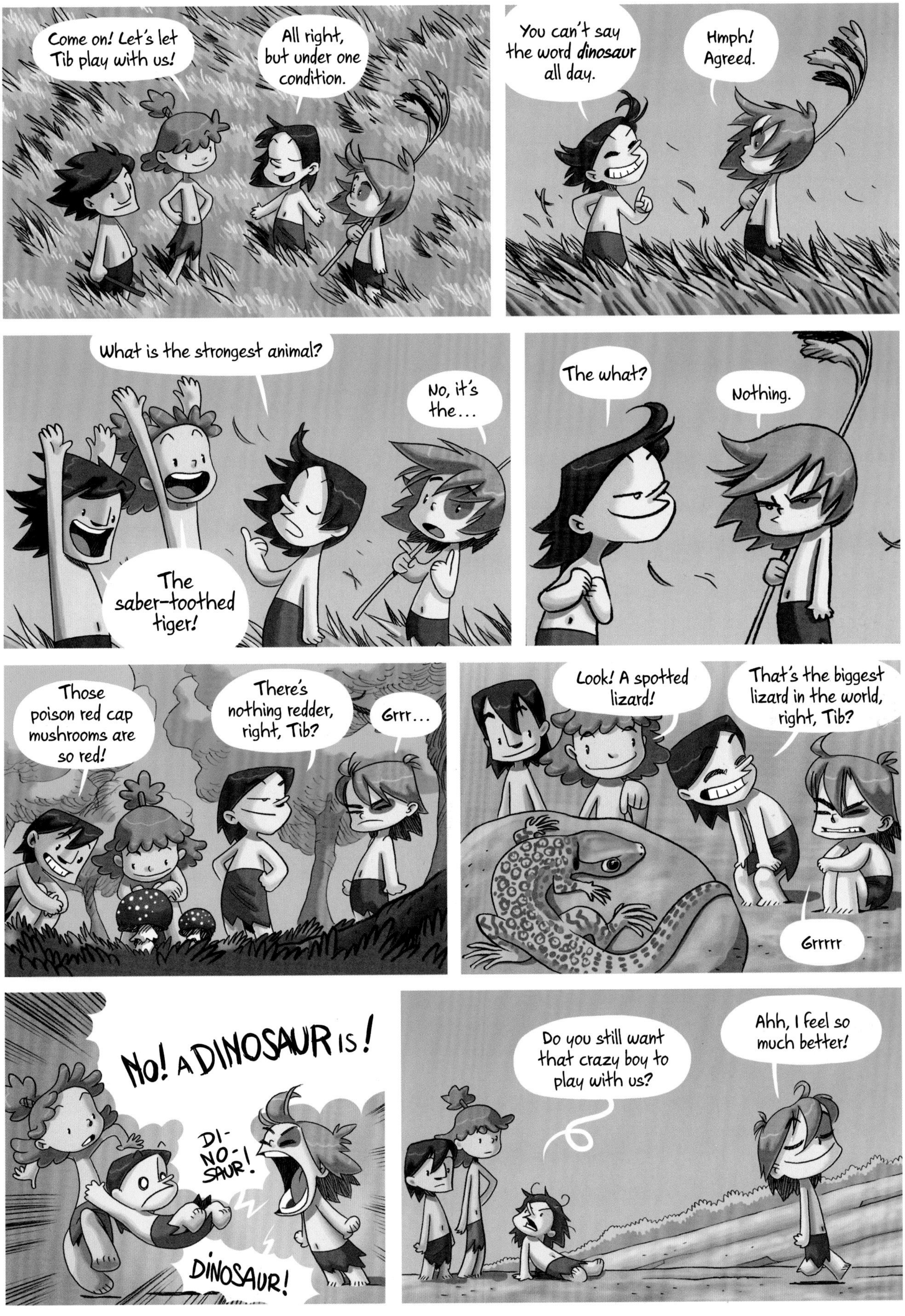

Come on! Let's let Tib play with us!
All right, but under one condition.
You can't say the word **dinosaur** all day.
Hmph! Agreed.
What is the strongest animal?
The saber-toothed tiger!
No, it's the...
The what?
Nothing.
Those poison red cap mushrooms are so red!
There's nothing redder, right, Tib?
Grrr...
Look! A spotted lizard!
That's the biggest lizard in the world, right, Tib?
Grrrrr
No! A DINOSAUR IS!
DI-NO-SAUR!
DINOSAUR!
Do you still want that crazy boy to play with us?
Ahh, I feel so much better!

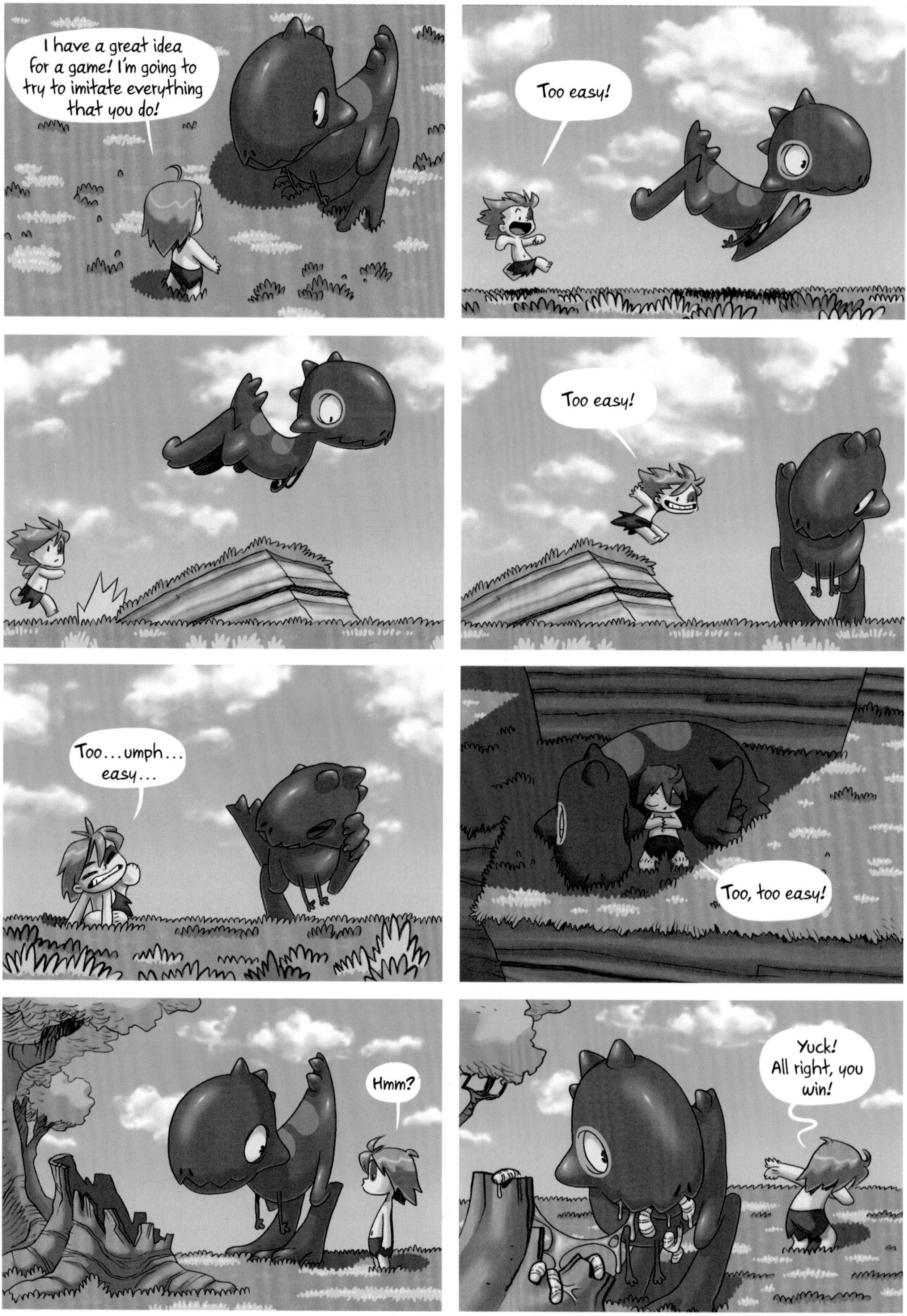
I have a great idea for a game! I'm going to try to imitate everything that you do!
Too easy!
Too easy!
Too... umph... easy...
Too, too easy!
Hmm?
Yuck! All right, you win!

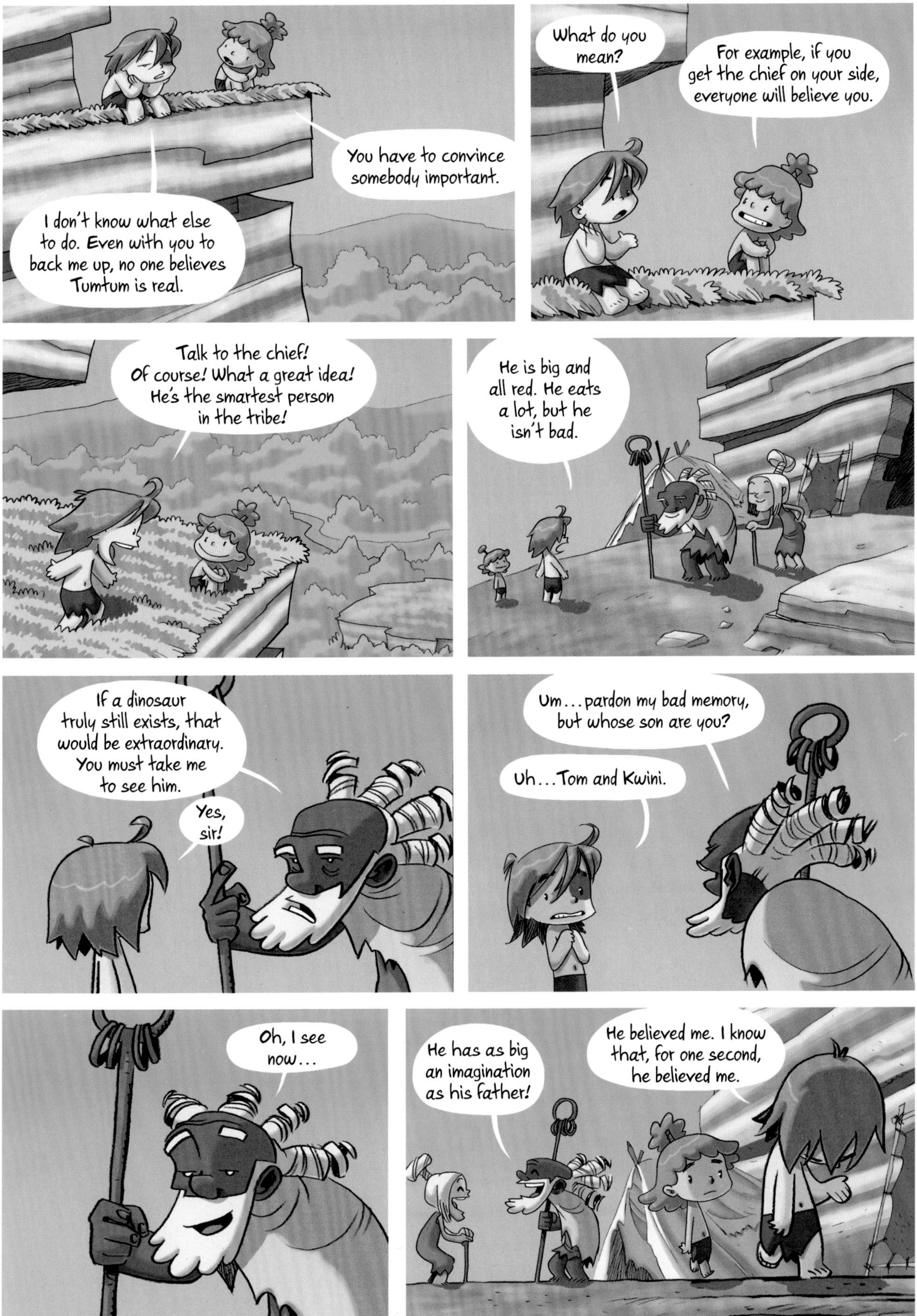
I don't know what else to do. Even with you to back me up, no one believes Tumtum is real.
You have to convince somebody important.
What do you mean?
For example, if you get the chief on your side, everyone will believe you.
Talk to the chief! Of course! What a great idea! He's the smartest person in the tribe!
He is big and all red. He eats a lot, but he isn't bad.
If a dinosaur truly still exists, that would be extraordinary. You must take me to see him.
Yes, sir!
Um... pardon my bad memory, but whose son are you?
Uh... Tom and Kwini.
Oh, I see now...
He has as big an imagination as his father!
He believed me. I know that, for one second, he believed me.

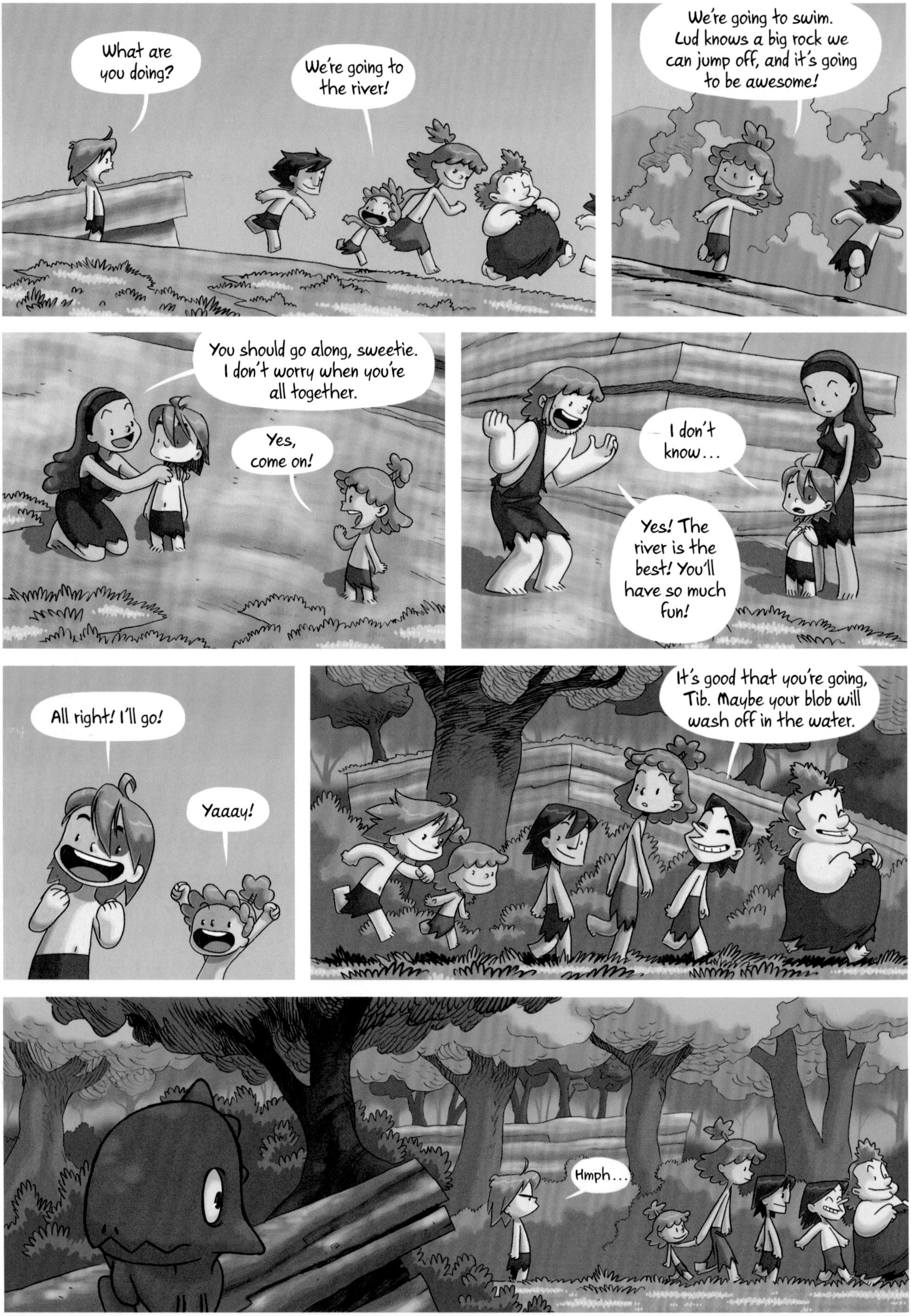
What are you doing?
We're going to the river!
We're going to swim. Lud knows a big rock we can jump off, and it's going to be awesome!
You should go along, sweetie. I don't worry when you're all together.
Yes, come on!
I don't know...
Yes! The river is the best! You'll have so much fun!
All right! I'll go!
Yaaay!
It's good that you're going, Tib. Maybe your blob will wash off in the water.
Hmph...

We're going to play "who can splash the biggest"!

Are you sure that's a good idea?

Tib is a chicken!

Yeehah!

Me next!

SPLOUTCH

I don't care. I'm too scared. I can't do it.

Woohoo!

Tumtum!

What are you doing?

Where are you going? Put me down!

AAAAAAAAHH

AAAAAAAAHH

SPLAAAASHH

Wow, I think he wins!

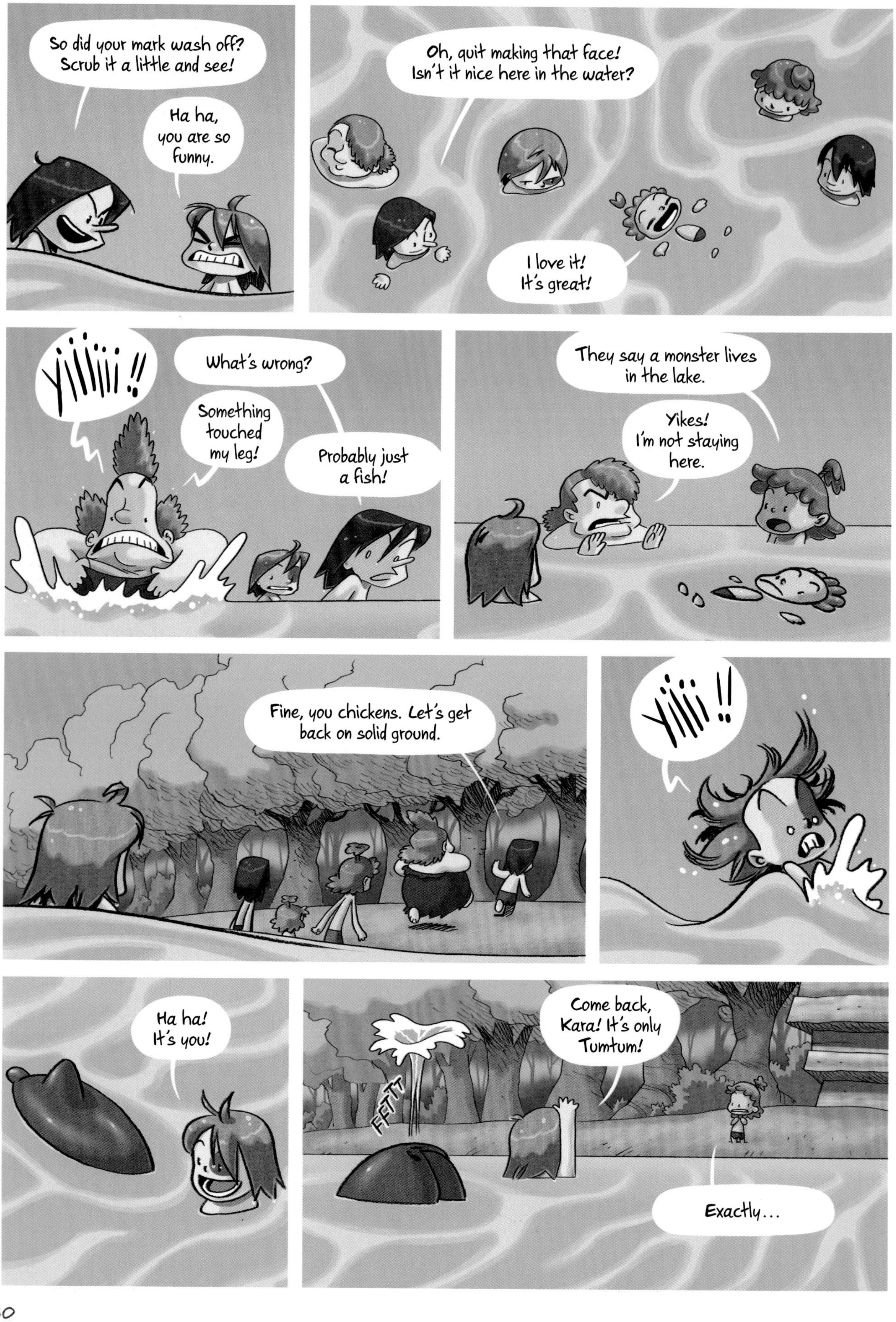

So did your mark wash off? Scrub it a little and see!
Ha ha, you are so funny.
Oh, quit making that face! Isn't it nice here in the water?
I love it! It's great!
Yiiiiii!!
What's wrong?
Something touched my leg!
Probably just a fish!
They say a monster lives in the lake.
Yikes! I'm not staying here.
Fine, you chickens. Let's get back on solid ground.
Yiiii!!
Ha ha! It's you!
FFTTT
Come back, Kara! It's only Tumtum!
Exactly...

So are you afraid to jump too?

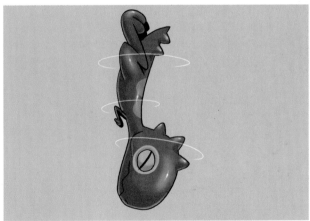

PLIP

Why do you say "he's showing off"? He's an animal, not a human.

You didn't see that dive!

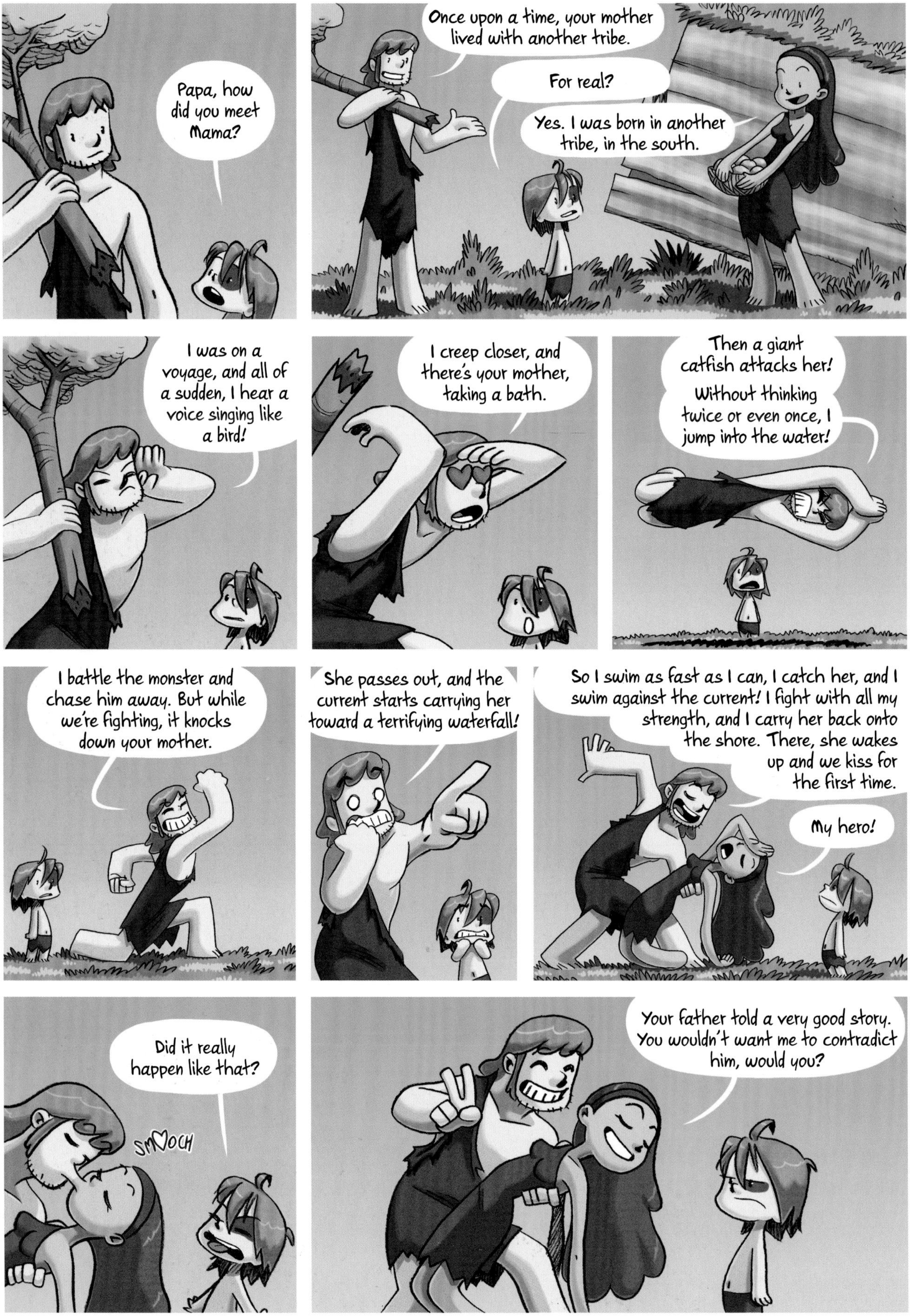

Papa, how did you meet Mama?
Once upon a time, your mother lived with another tribe.
For real?
Yes. I was born in another tribe, in the south.
I was on a voyage, and all of a sudden, I hear a voice singing like a bird!
I creep closer, and there's your mother, taking a bath.
Then a giant catfish attacks her!
Without thinking twice or even once, I jump into the water!
I battle the monster and chase him away. But while we're fighting, it knocks down your mother.
She passes out, and the current starts carrying her toward a terrifying waterfall!
So I swim as fast as I can, I catch her, and I swim against the current! I fight with all my strength, and I carry her back onto the shore. There, she wakes up and we kiss for the first time.
My hero!
Did it really happen like that?
SMOOCH
Your father told a very good story. You wouldn't want me to contradict him, would you?

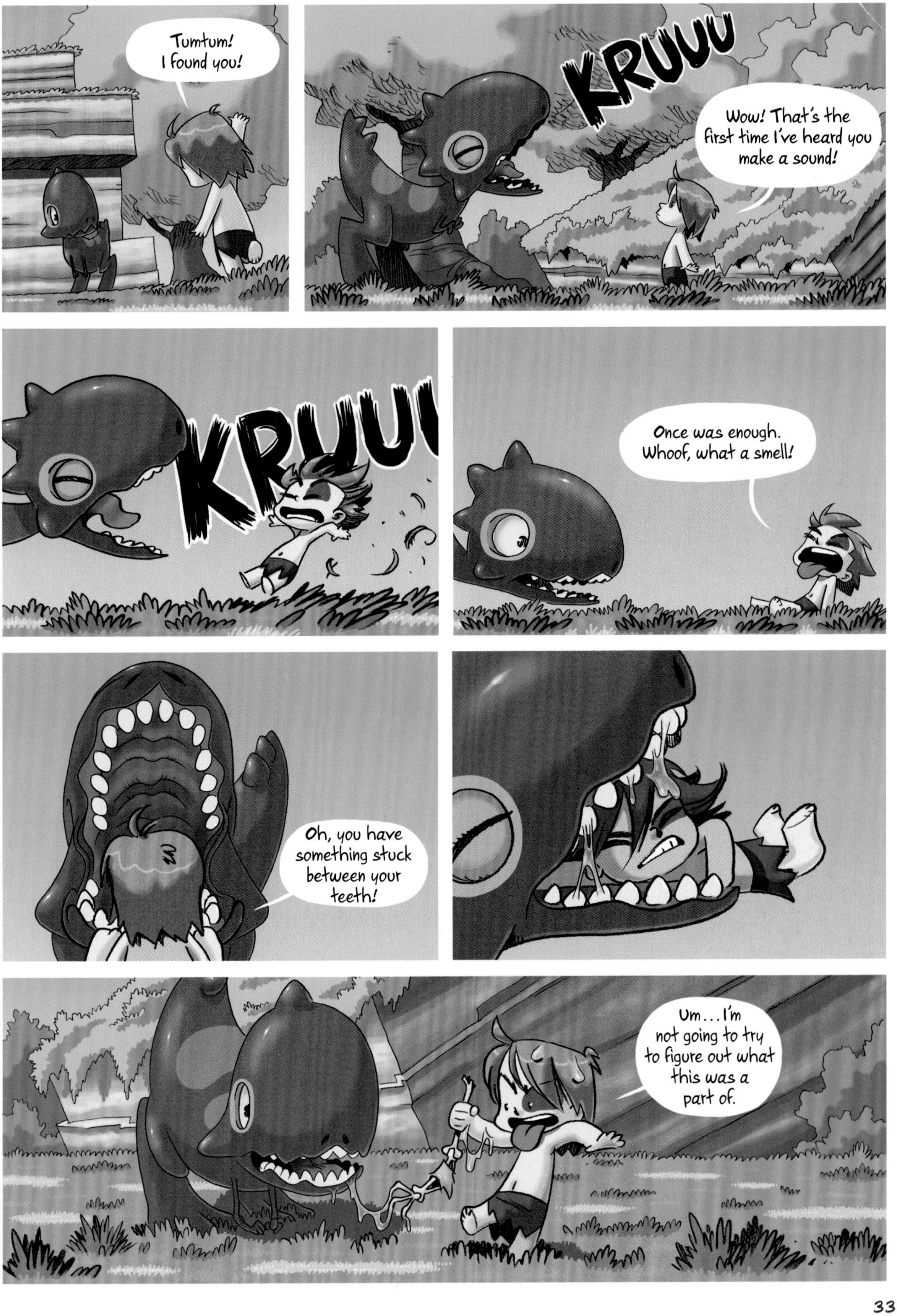
Tumtum! I found you!
KRUUU
Wow! That's the first time I've heard you make a sound!
KRUUU
Once was enough. Whoof, what a smell!
Oh, you have something stuck between your teeth!
Um... I'm not going to try to figure out what this was a part of.

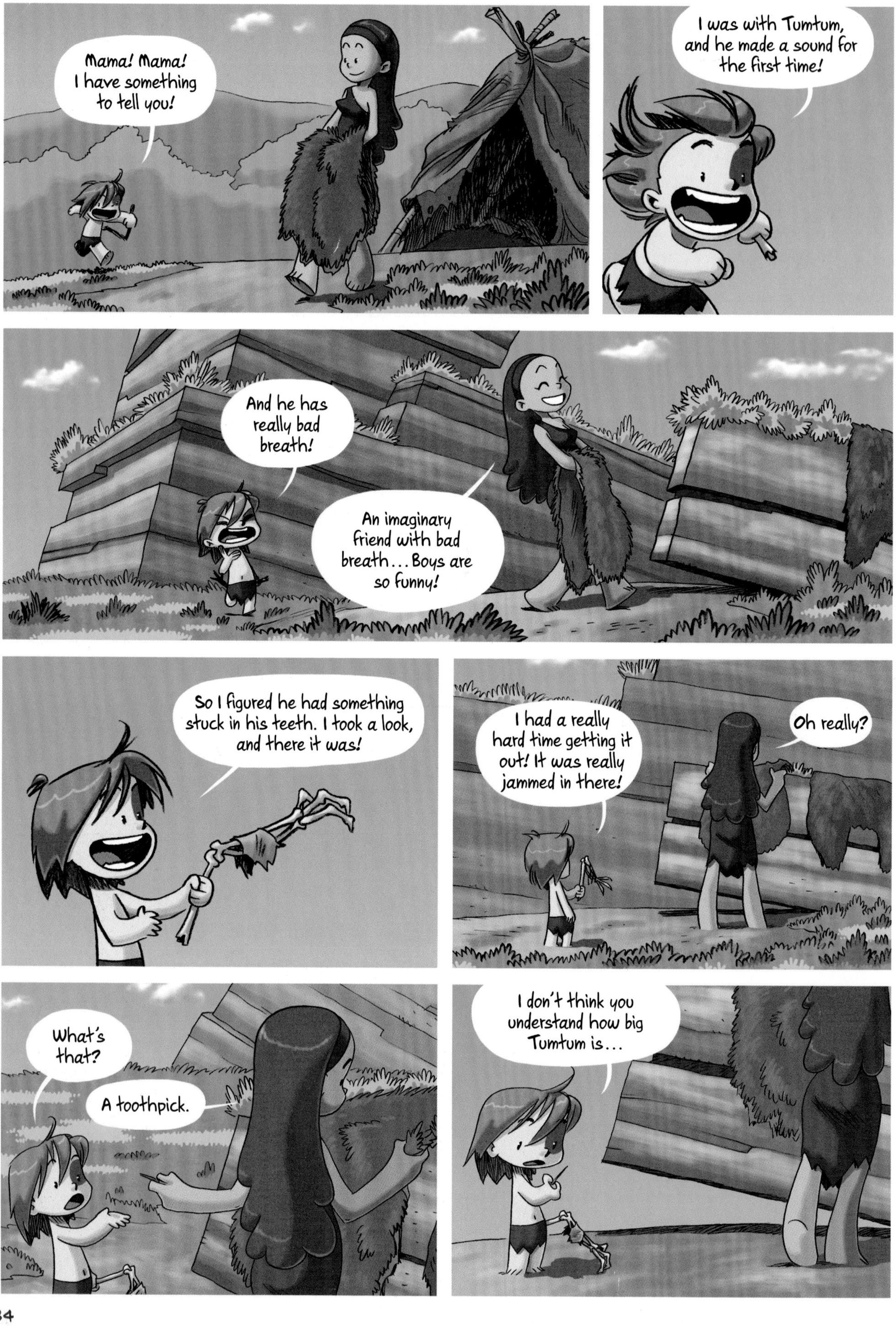

Mama! Mama! I have something to tell you!
I was with Tumtum, and he made a sound for the first time!
And he has really bad breath!
An imaginary friend with bad breath... Boys are so funny!
So I figured he had something stuck in his teeth. I took a look, and there it was!
I had a really hard time getting it out! It was really jammed in there!
Oh really?
What's that?
A toothpick.
I don't think you understand how big Tumtum is...

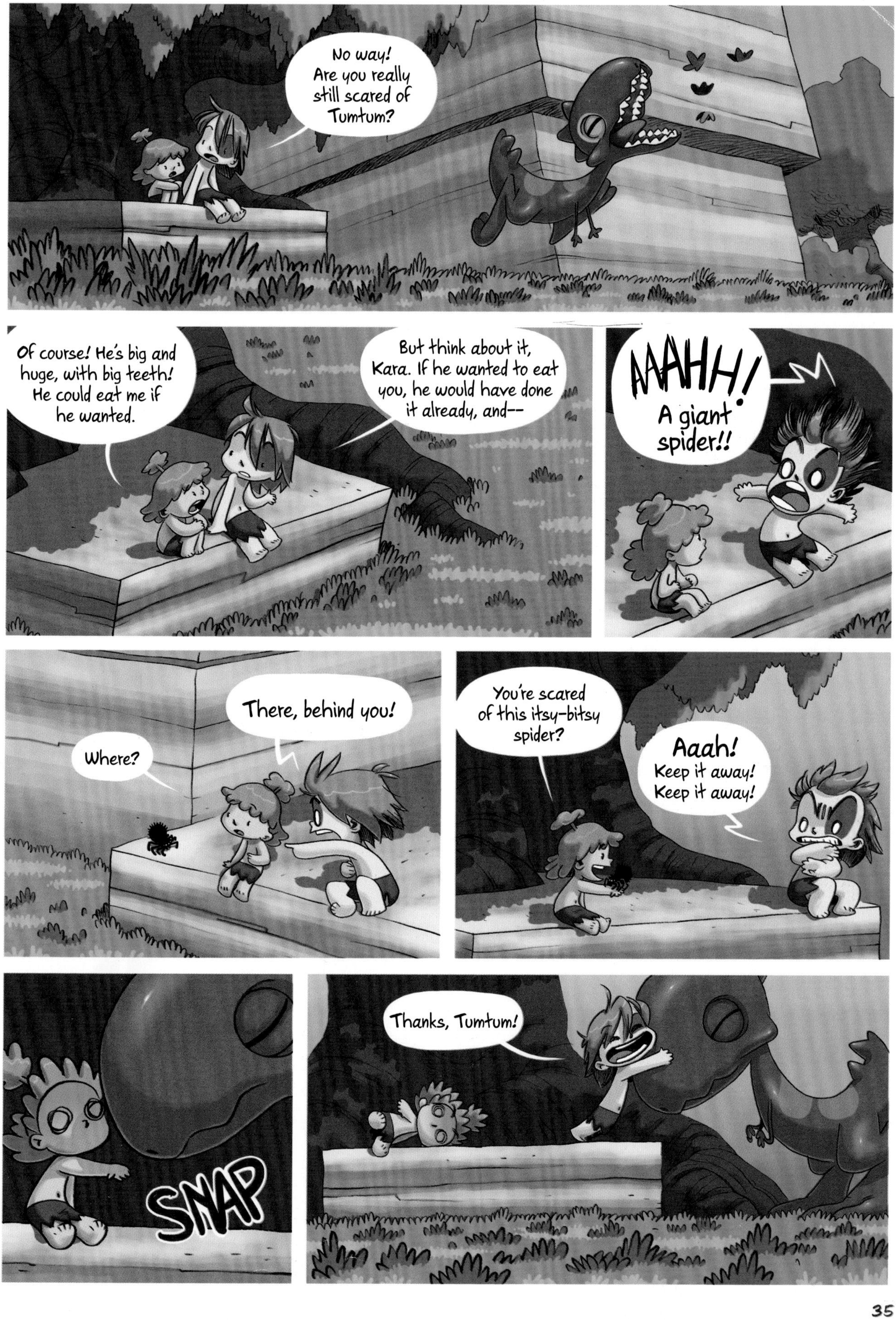
No way! Are you really still scared of Tumtum?
Of course! He's big and huge, with big teeth! He could eat me if he wanted.
But think about it, Kara. If he wanted to eat you, he would have done it already, and--
AAAHH! A giant spider!!
Where?
There, behind you!
You're scared of this itsy-bitsy spider?
Aaah! Keep it away! Keep it away!
SNAP
Thanks, Tumtum!

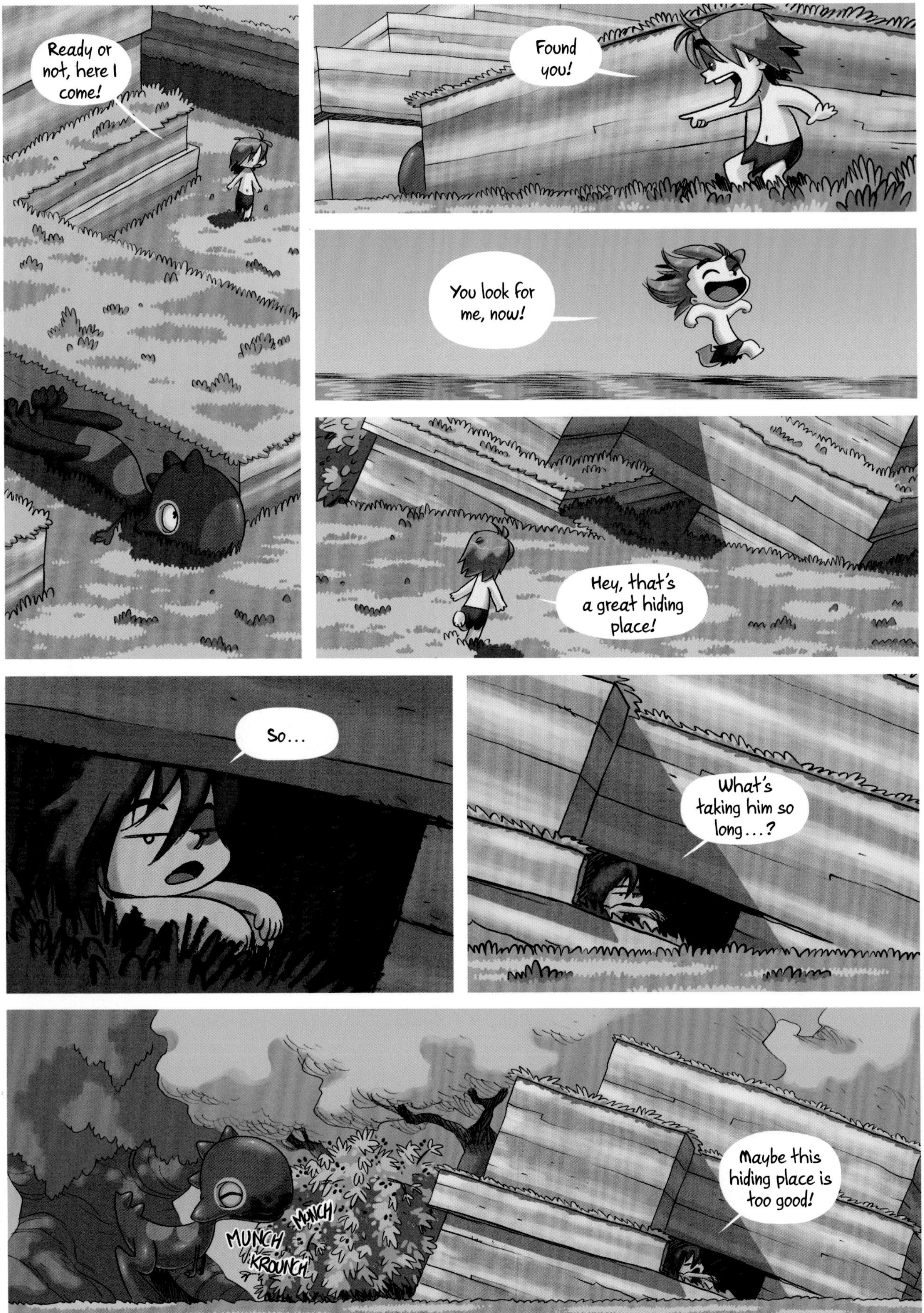
Ready or not, here I come!
Found you!
You look for me, now!
Hey, that's a great hiding place!
So...
What's taking him so long...?
MUNCH
MUNCH
KROUNCH
Maybe this hiding place is too good!

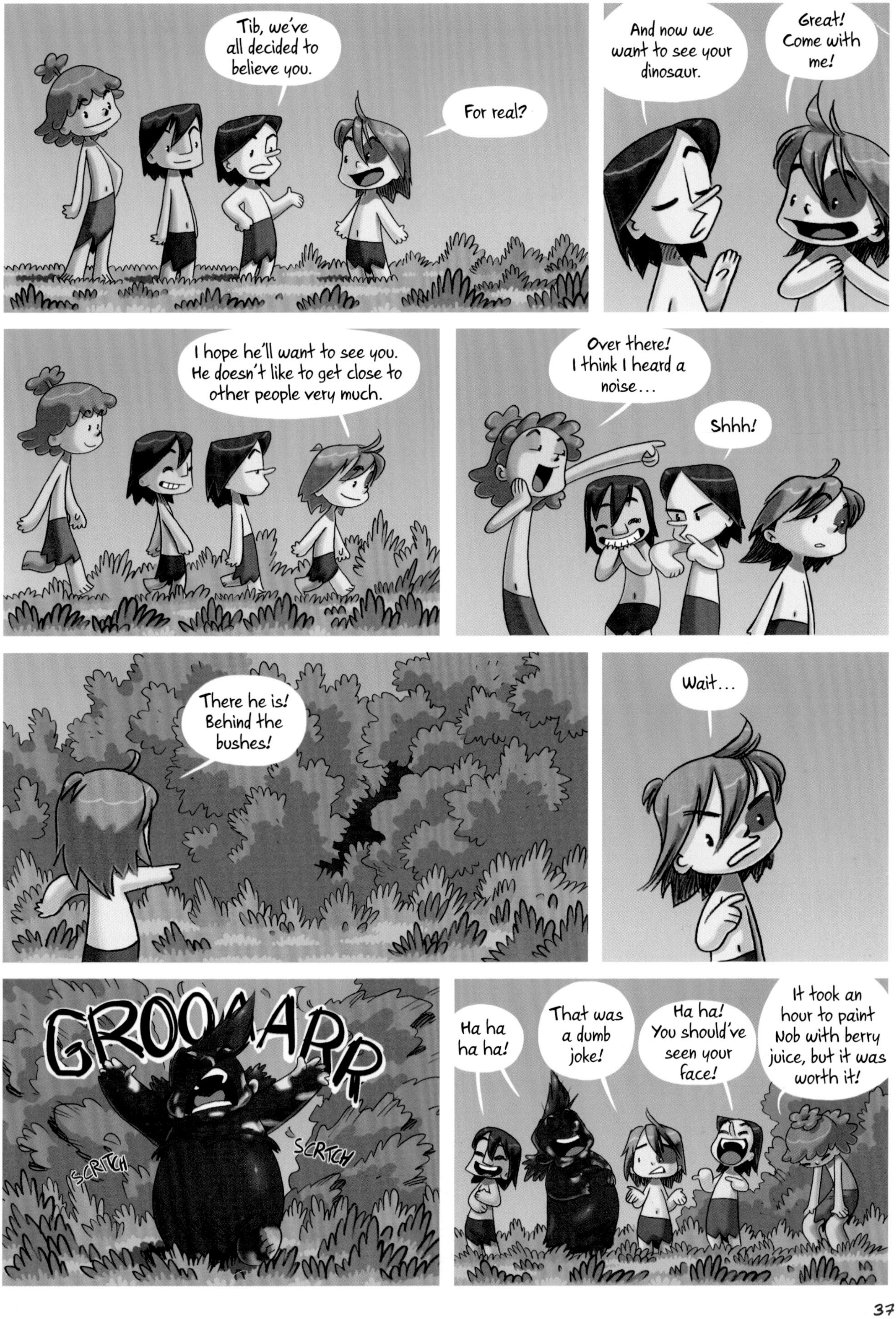
Tib, we've all decided to believe you.
For real?
And now we want to see your dinosaur.
Great! Come with me!
I hope he'll want to see you. He doesn't like to get close to other people very much.
Over there! I think I heard a noise...
Shhh!
There he is! Behind the bushes!
Wait...
GROOAARR
SCRTCH
SCRTCH
Ha ha ha ha!
That was a dumb joke!
Ha ha! You should've seen your face!
It took an hour to paint Nob with berry juice, but it was worth it!

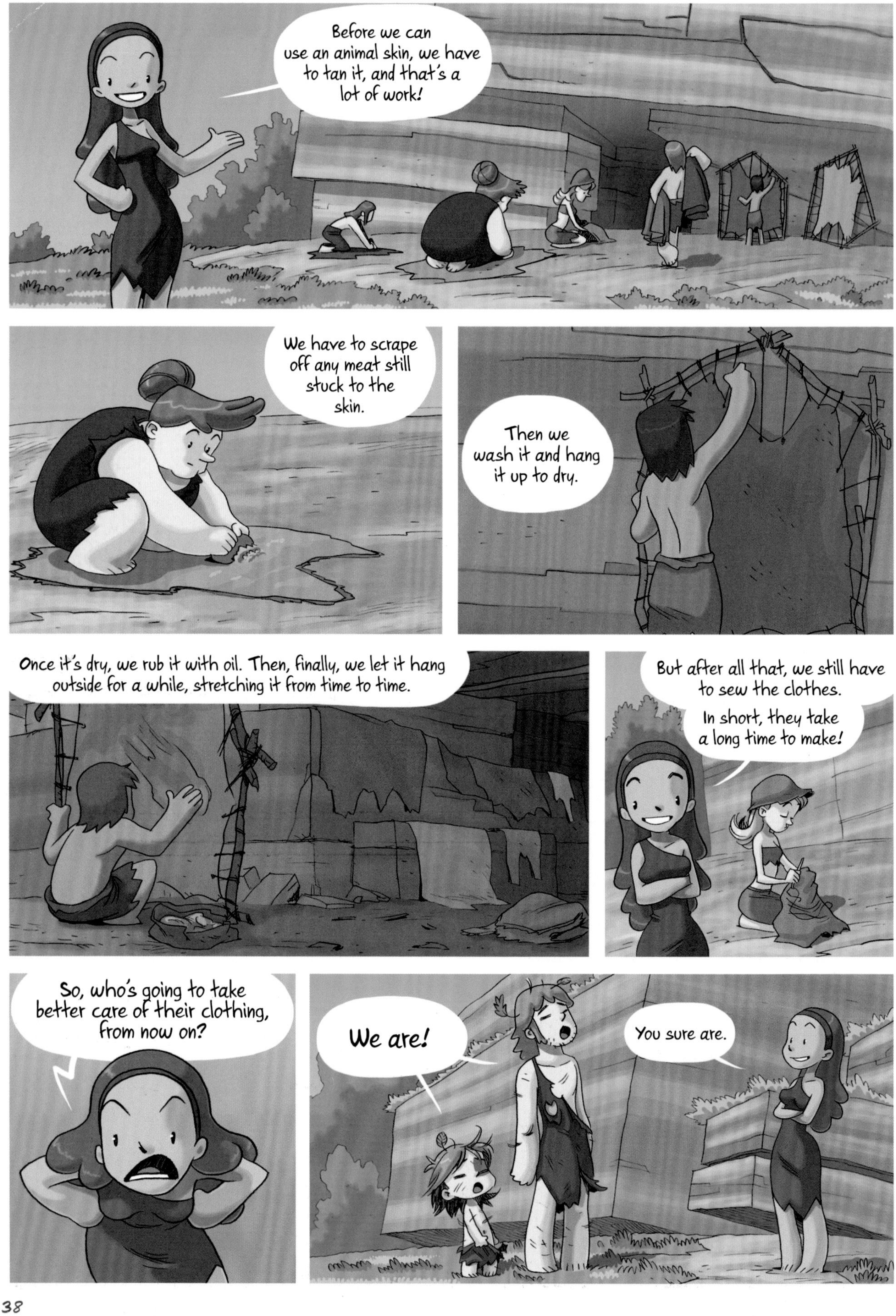

Before we can use an animal skin, we have to tan it, and that's a lot of work!
We have to scrape off any meat still stuck to the skin.
Then we wash it and hang it up to dry.
Once it's dry, we rub it with oil. Then, finally, we let it hang outside for a while, stretching it from time to time.
But after all that, we still have to sew the clothes.
In short, they take a long time to make!
So, who's going to take better care of their clothing, from now on?
We are!
You sure are.

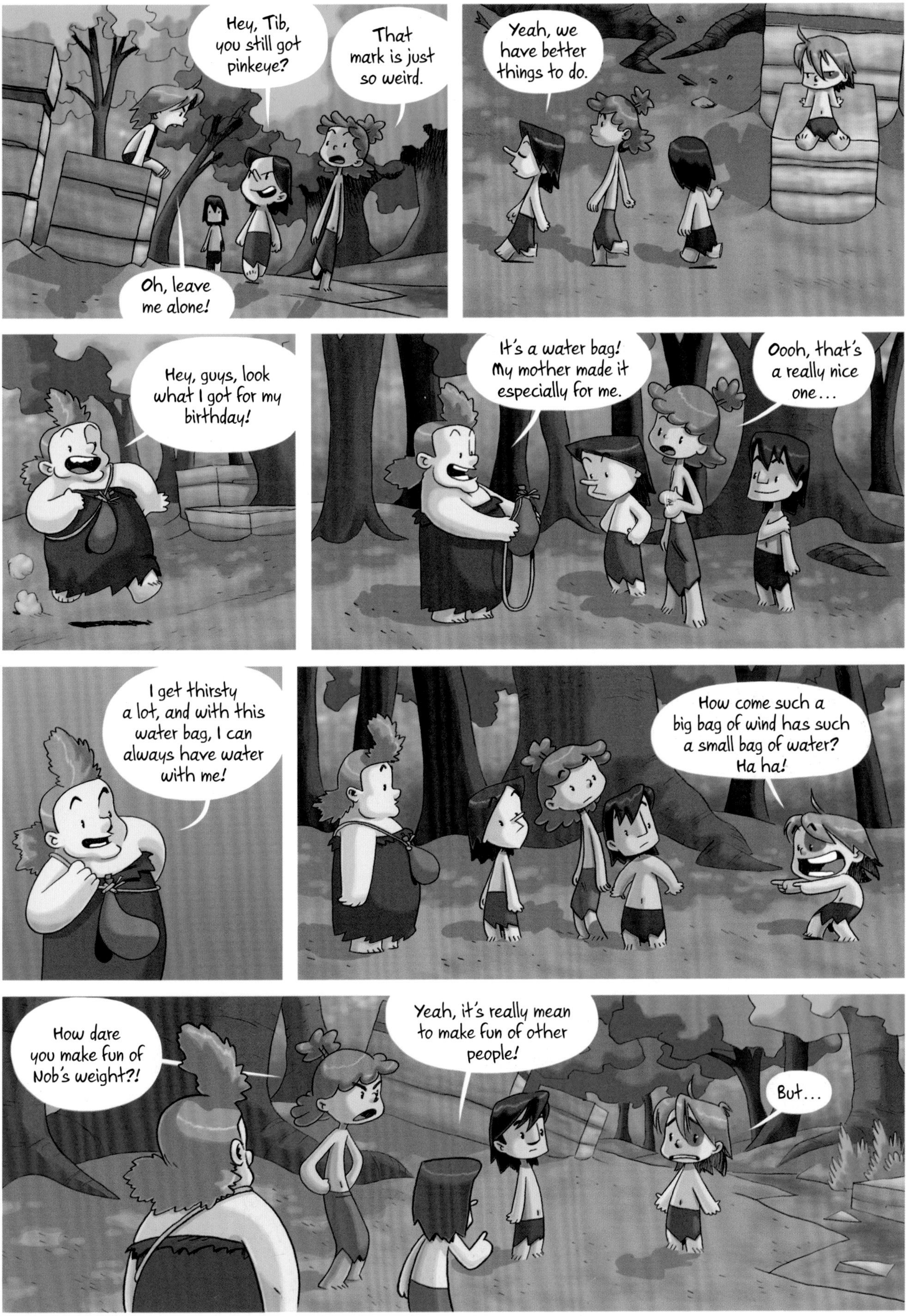
Hey, Tib, you still got pinkeye?
That mark is just so weird.
Oh, leave me alone!
Yeah, we have better things to do.
Hey, guys, look what I got for my birthday!
It's a water bag! My mother made it especially for me.
Oooh, that's a really nice one...
I get thirsty a lot, and with this water bag, I can always have water with me!
How come such a big bag of wind has such a small bag of water? Ha ha!
How dare you make fun of Nob's weight?!
Yeah, it's really mean to make fun of other people!
But...

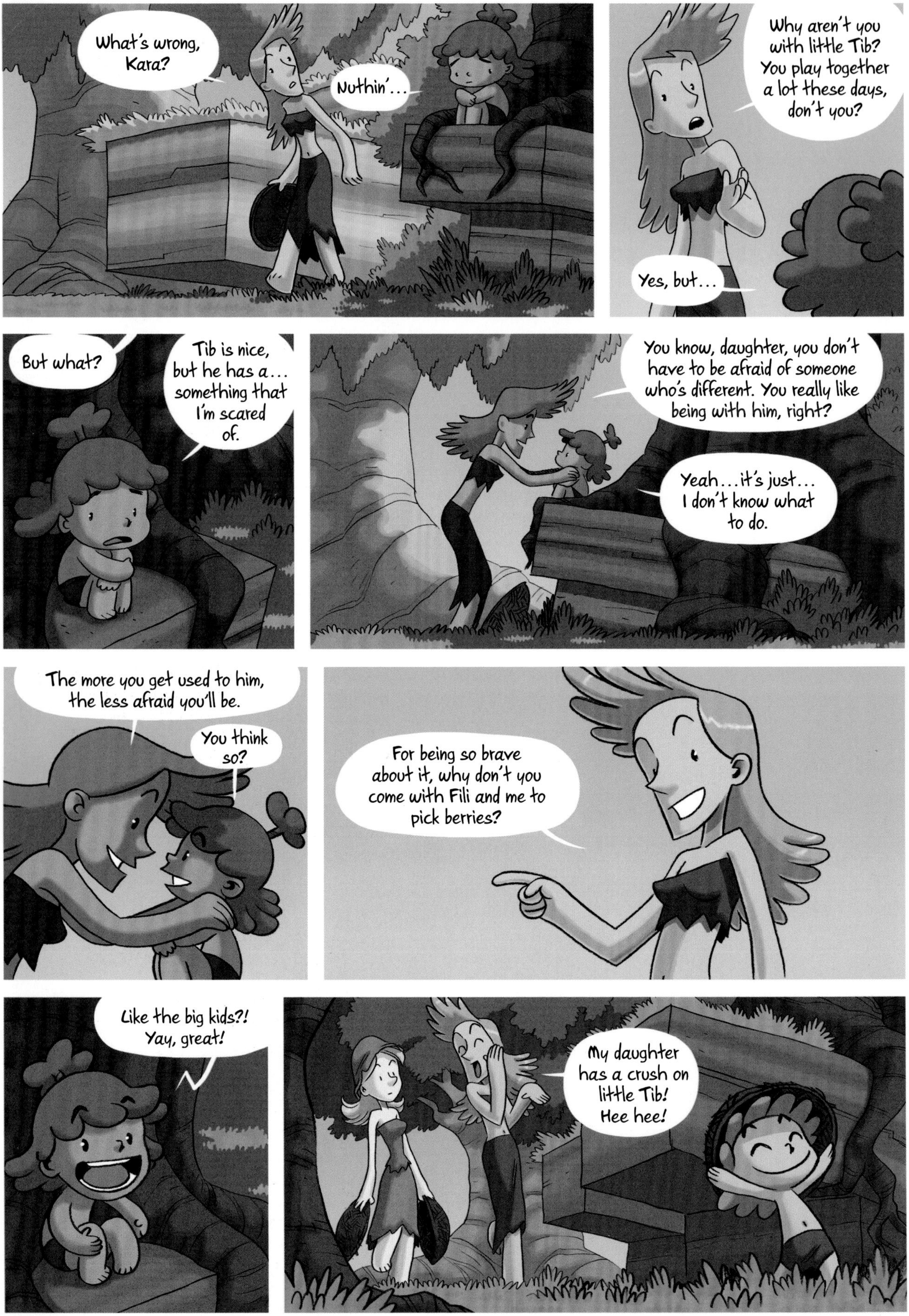
What's wrong, Kara?
Nuthin'...
Why aren't you with little Tib? You play together a lot these days, don't you?
Yes, but...
But what?
Tib is nice, but he has a... something that I'm scared of.
You know, daughter, you don't have to be afraid of someone who's different. You really like being with him, right?
Yeah...it's just... I don't know what to do.
The more you get used to him, the less afraid you'll be.
You think so?
For being so brave about it, why don't you come with Fili and me to pick berries?
Like the big kids?! Yay, great!
My daughter has a crush on little Tib! Hee hee!

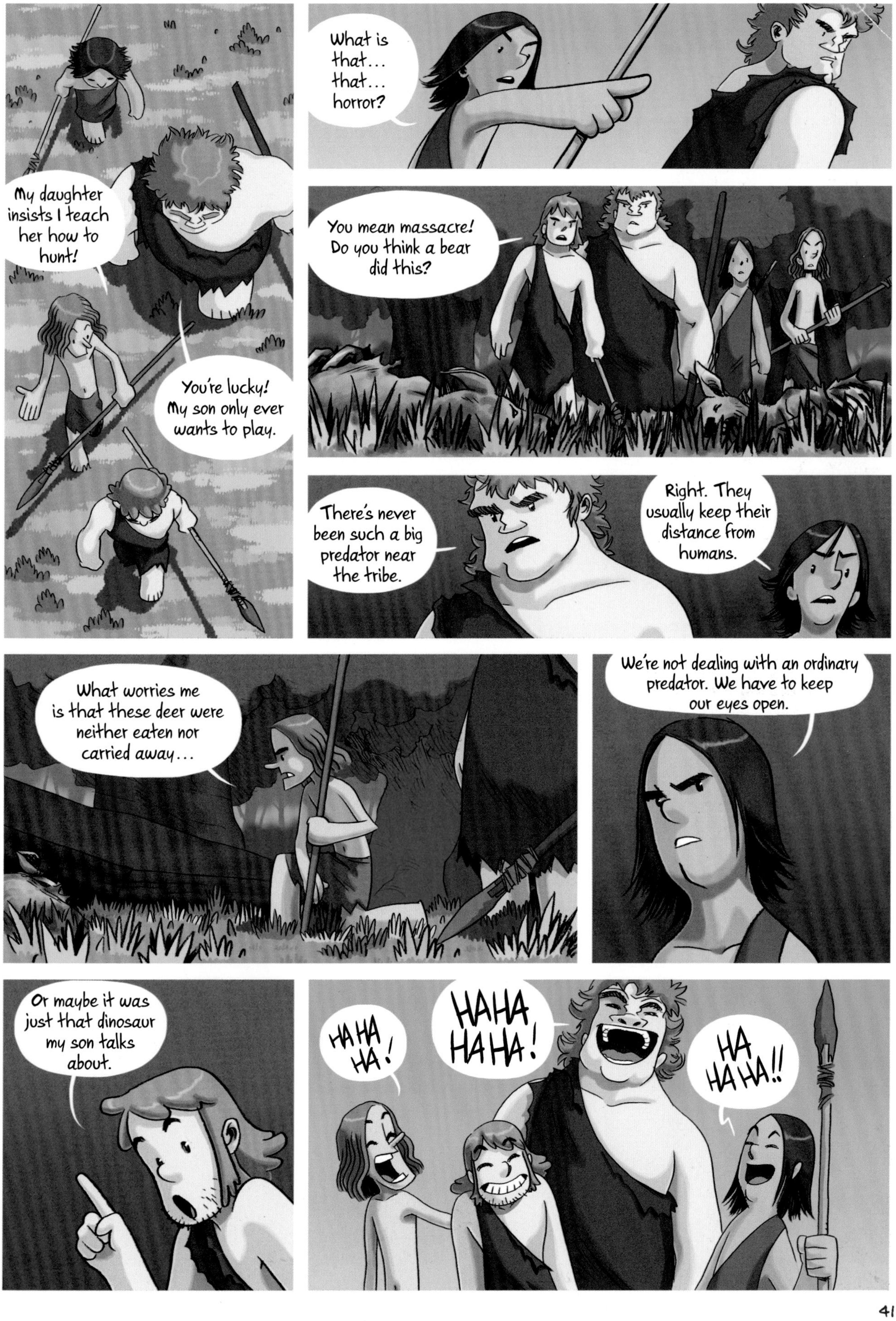

My daughter insists I teach her how to hunt!
You're lucky! My son only ever wants to play.
What is that… that… horror?
You mean massacre! Do you think a bear did this?
There's never been such a big predator near the tribe.
Right. They usually keep their distance from humans.
What worries me is that these deer were neither eaten nor carried away…
We're not dealing with an ordinary predator. We have to keep our eyes open.
Or maybe it was just that dinosaur my son talks about.
HA HA HA!
HAHA HAHA!
HA HAHA!!

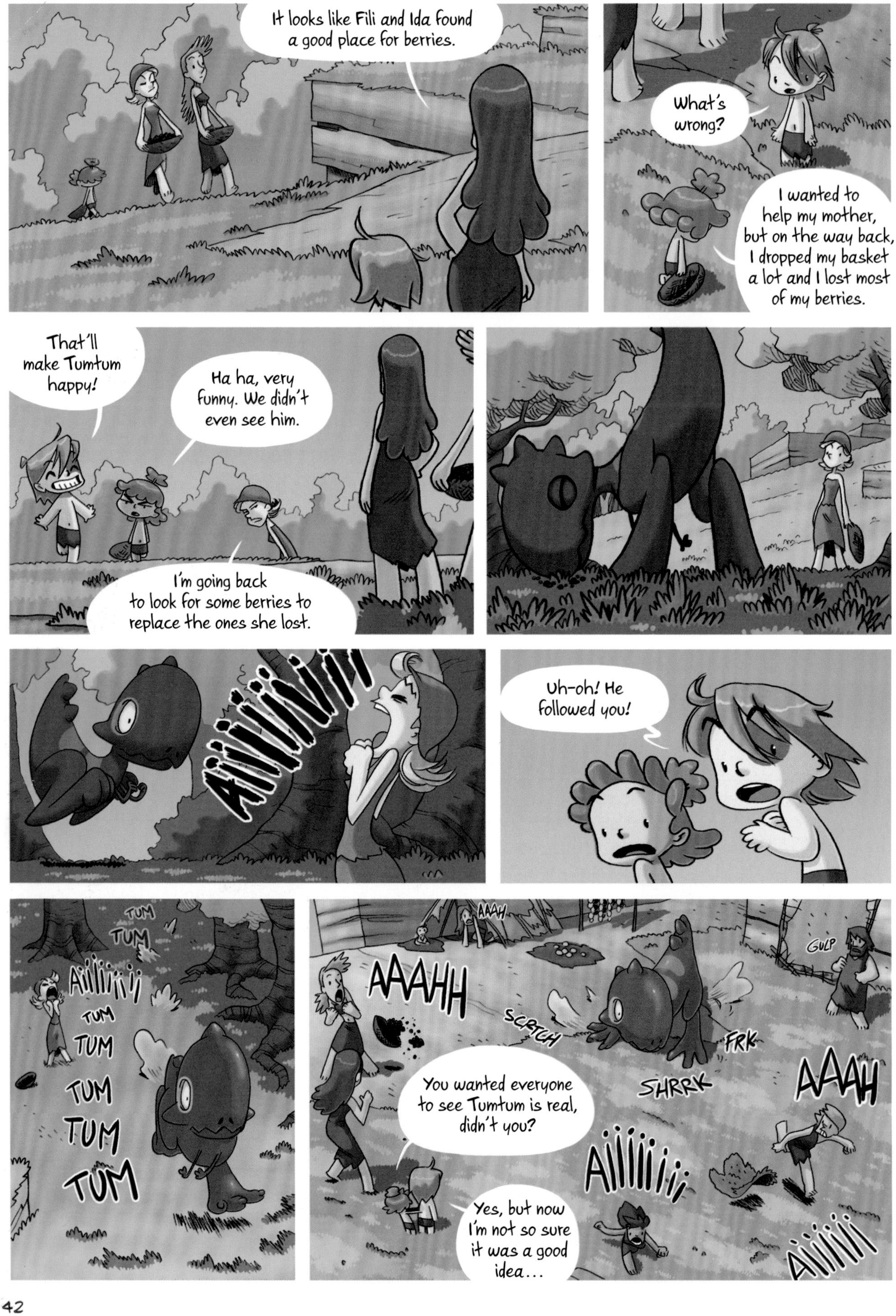
It looks like Fili and Ida found a good place for berries.
What's wrong?
I wanted to help my mother, but on the way back, I dropped my basket a lot and I lost most of my berries.
That'll make Tumtum happy!
Ha ha, very funny. We didn't even see him.
I'm going back to look for some berries to replace the ones she lost.
AIIIIIIIIIII
Uh-oh! He followed you!
TUM
TUM
AIIIIIII
TUM
TUM
TUM
TUM
TUM
AAAH
AAAHH
SCRTCH
GULP
FRK
SHRRK
AAAH
You wanted everyone to see Tumtum is real, didn't you?
AIIIIIII
Yes, but now I'm not so sure it was a good idea...
AIIIIII

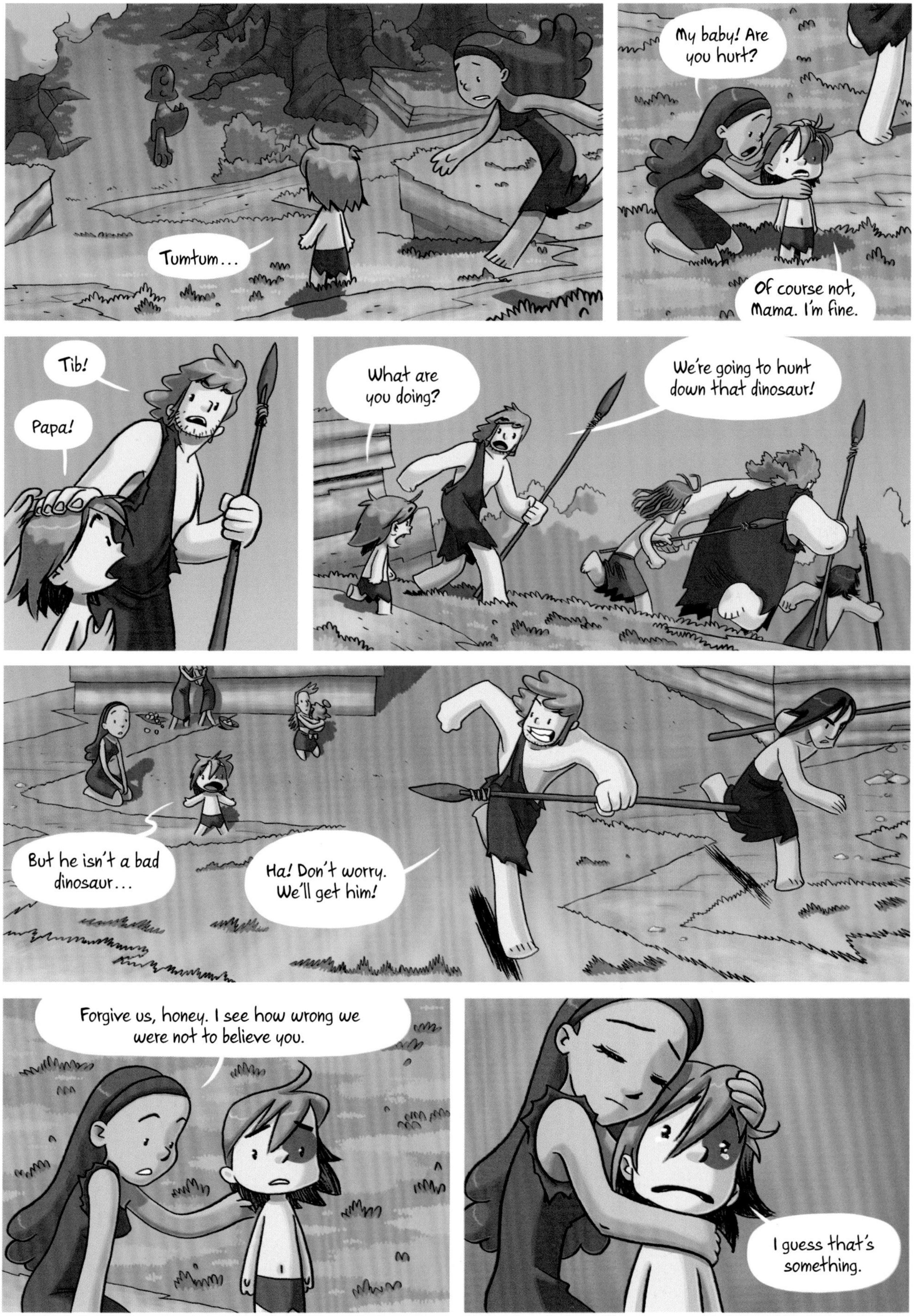
Tumtum...
My baby! Are you hurt?
Of course not, Mama. I'm fine.
Tib!
Papa!
What are you doing?
We're going to hunt down that dinosaur!
But he isn't a bad dinosaur...
Ha! Don't worry. We'll get him!
Forgive us, honey. I see how wrong we were not to believe you.
I guess that's something.

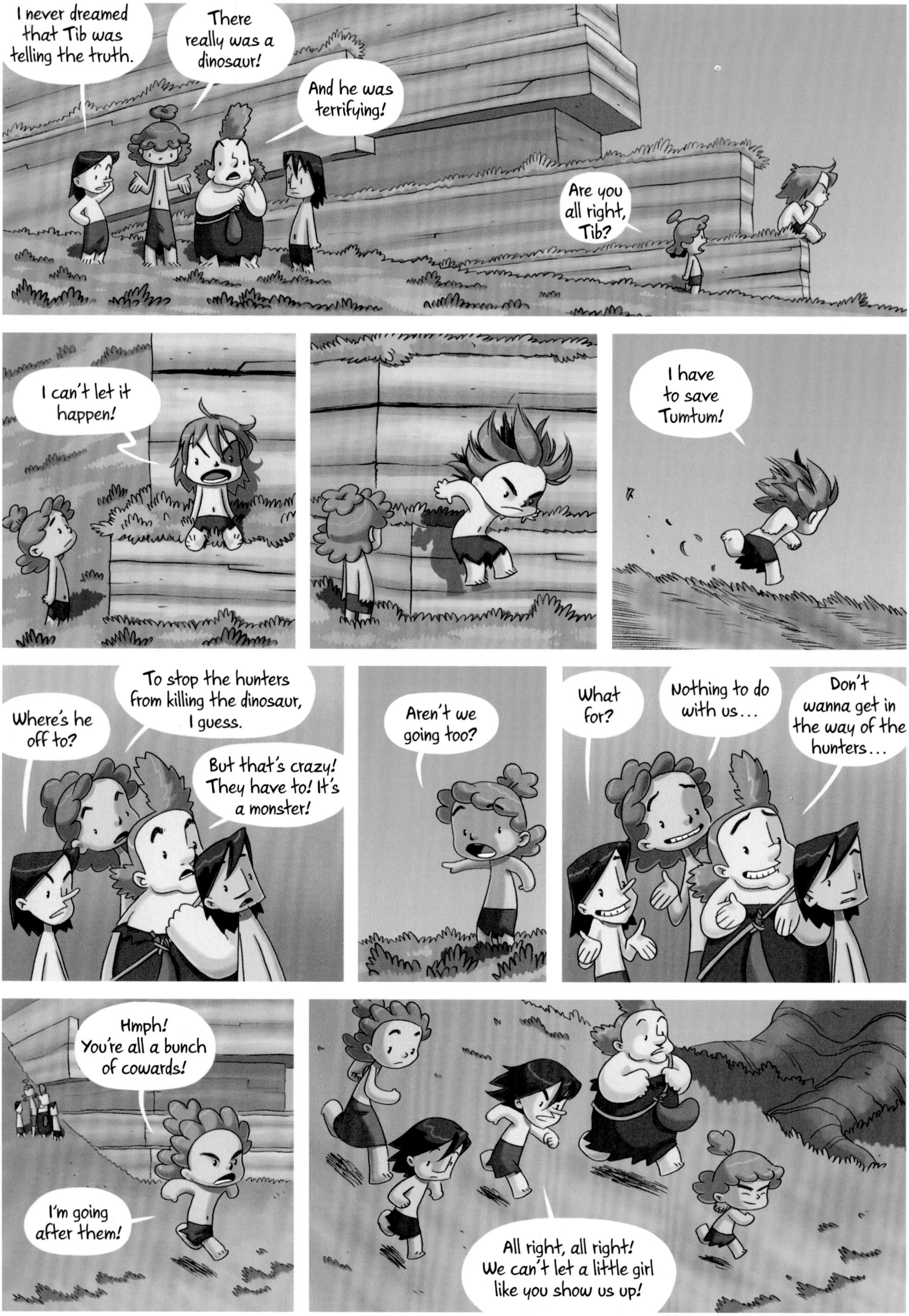
I never dreamed that Tib was telling the truth.
There really was a dinosaur!
And he was terrifying!
Are you all right, Tib?
I can't let it happen!
I have to save Tumtum!
Where's he off to?
To stop the hunters from killing the dinosaur, I guess.
But that's crazy! They have to! It's a monster!
Aren't we going too?
What for?
Nothing to do with us...
Don't wanna get in the way of the hunters...
Hmph! You're all a bunch of cowards!
I'm going after them!
All right, all right! We can't let a little girl like you show us up!

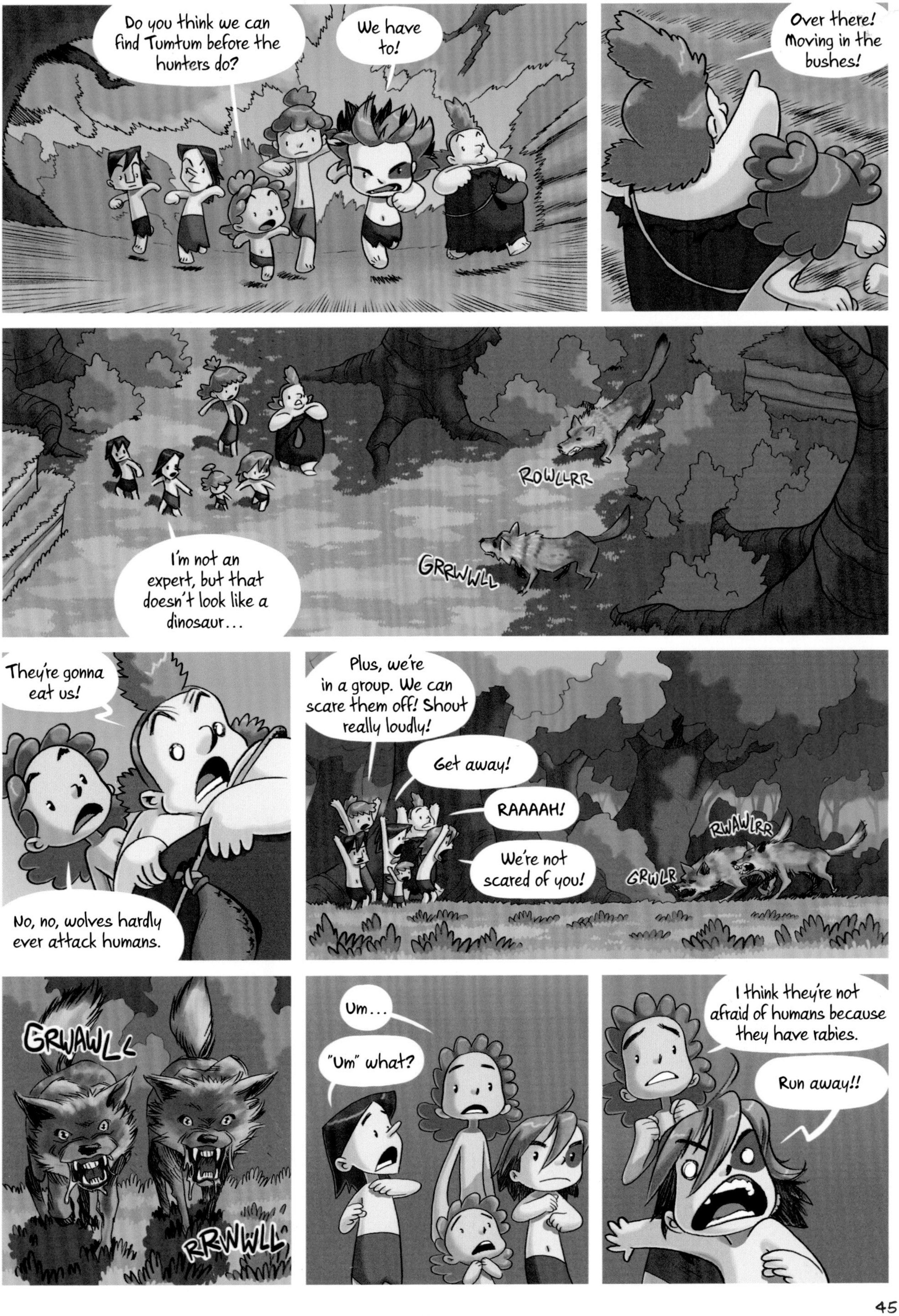
Do you think we can find Tumtum before the hunters do?
We have to!
Over there! Moving in the bushes!
ROWLLRR
GRRWWLL
I'm not an expert, but that doesn't look like a dinosaur...
They're gonna eat us!
No, no, wolves hardly ever attack humans.
Plus, we're in a group. We can scare them off! Shout really loudly!
Get away!
RAAAAH!
We're not scared of you!
RWAWLRR
GRWLR
GRWAWLL
RRWWLL
Um...
"Um" what?
I think they're not afraid of humans because they have rabies.
Run away!!

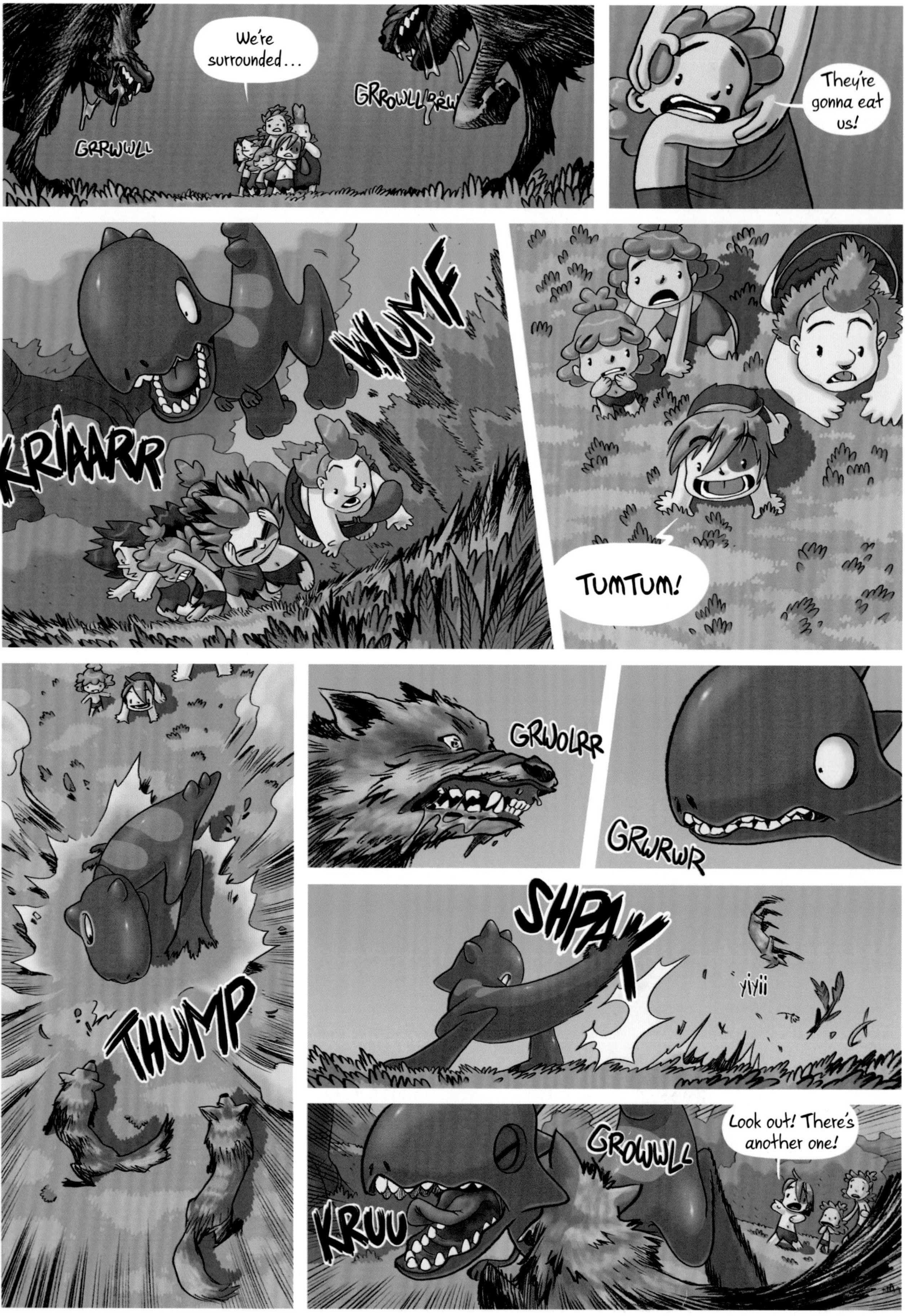
We're surrounded...
GRRWWLL
GRROWLLGRW
They're gonna eat us!
WUMF
KRIAARR
TUMTUM!
THUMP
GRWOLRR
GRWRWR
SHPAK
yiyii
GROWWLL
KRUU
Look out! There's another one!

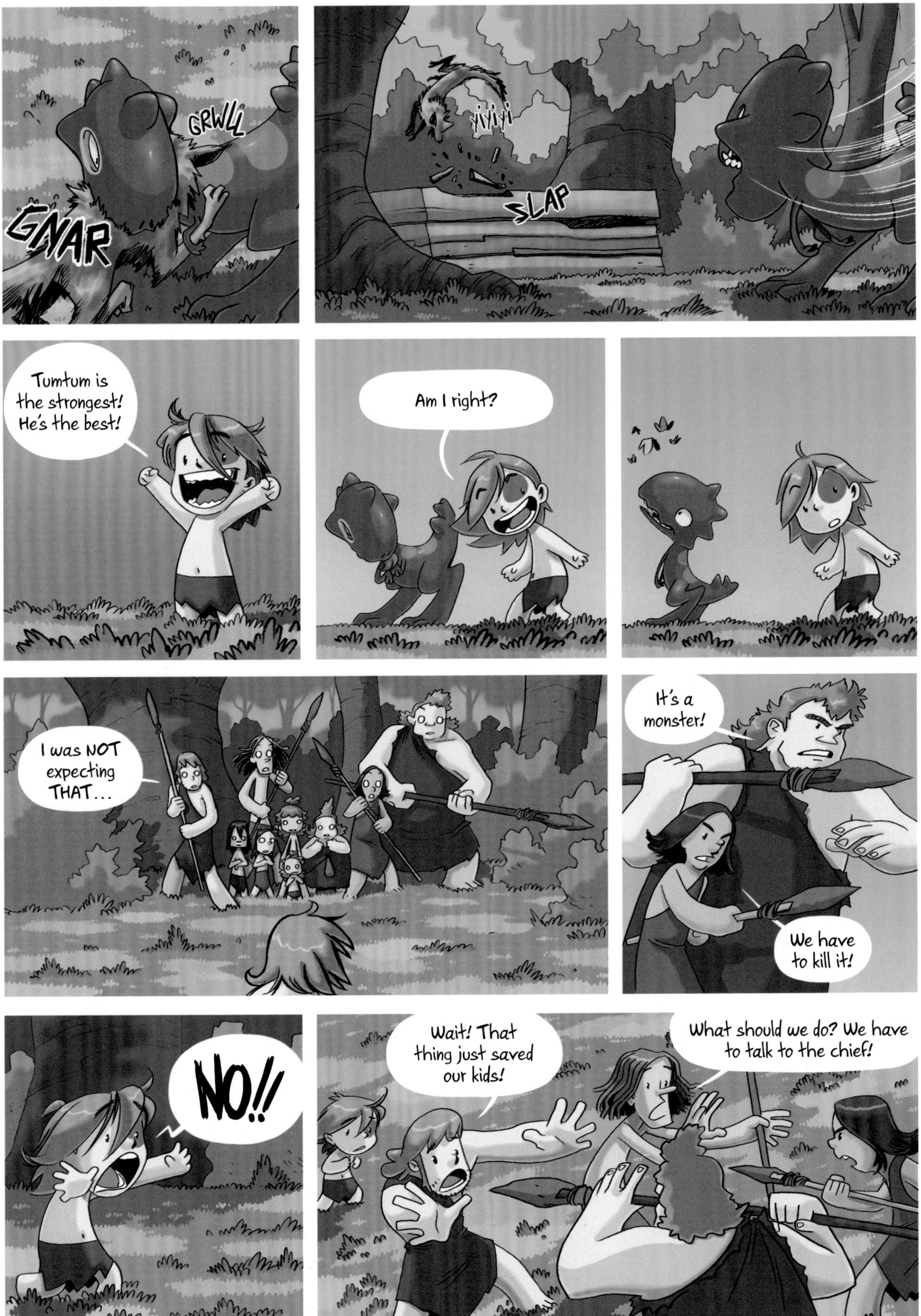
GRWLL
GNAR
YIYIYI
SLAP
Tumtum is the strongest! He's the best!
Am I right?
I was NOT expecting THAT...
It's a monster!
We have to kill it!
NO!!
Wait! That thing just saved our kids!
What should we do? We have to talk to the chief!

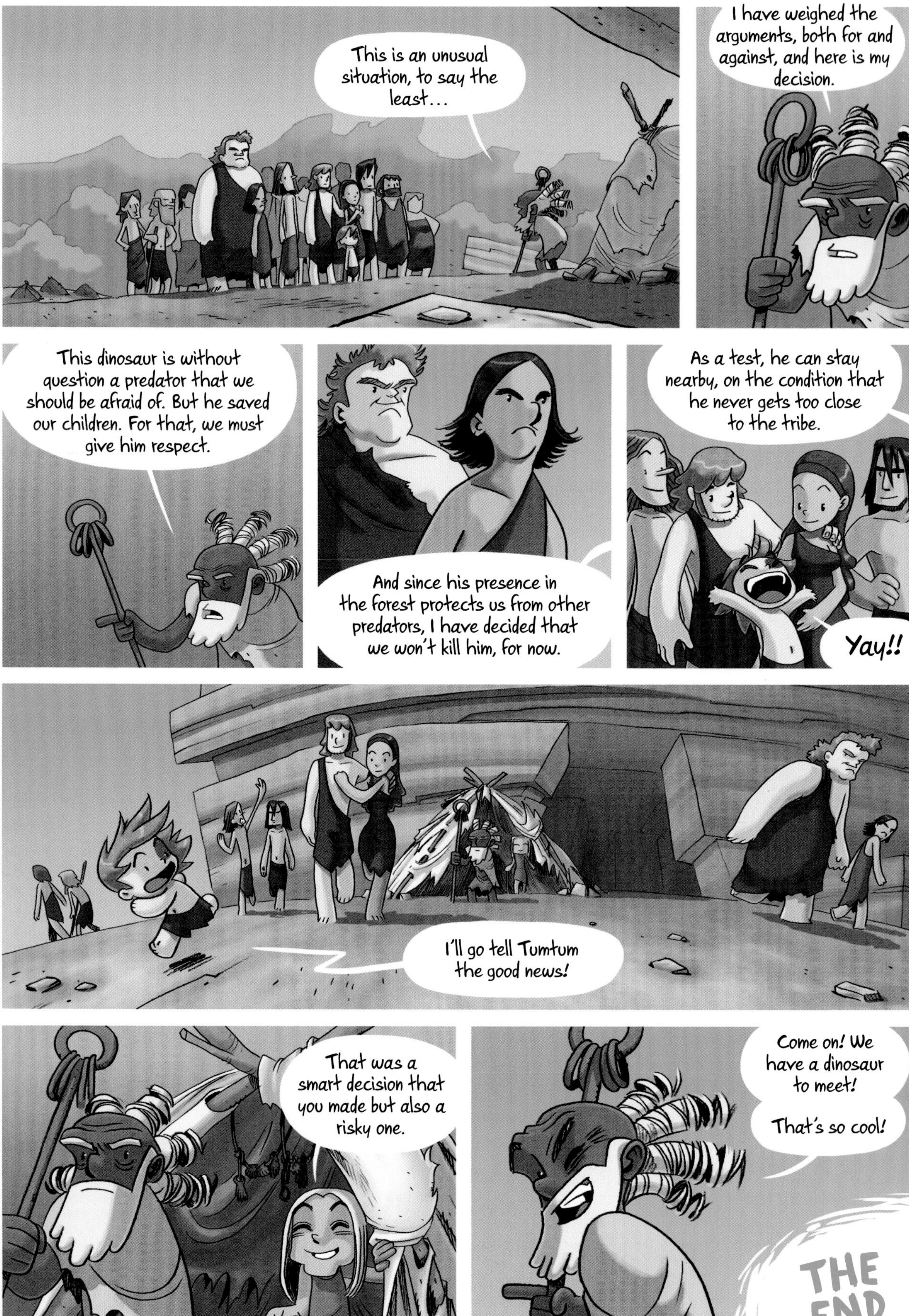
This is an unusual situation, to say the least...
I have weighed the arguments, both for and against, and here is my decision.
This dinosaur is without question a predator that we should be afraid of. But he saved our children. For that, we must give him respect.
And since his presence in the forest protects us from other predators, I have decided that we won't kill him, for now.
As a test, he can stay nearby, on the condition that he never gets too close to the tribe.
Yay!!
I'll go tell Tumtum the good news!
That was a smart decision that you made but also a risky one.
Come on! We have a dinosaur to meet!
That's so cool!
THE END

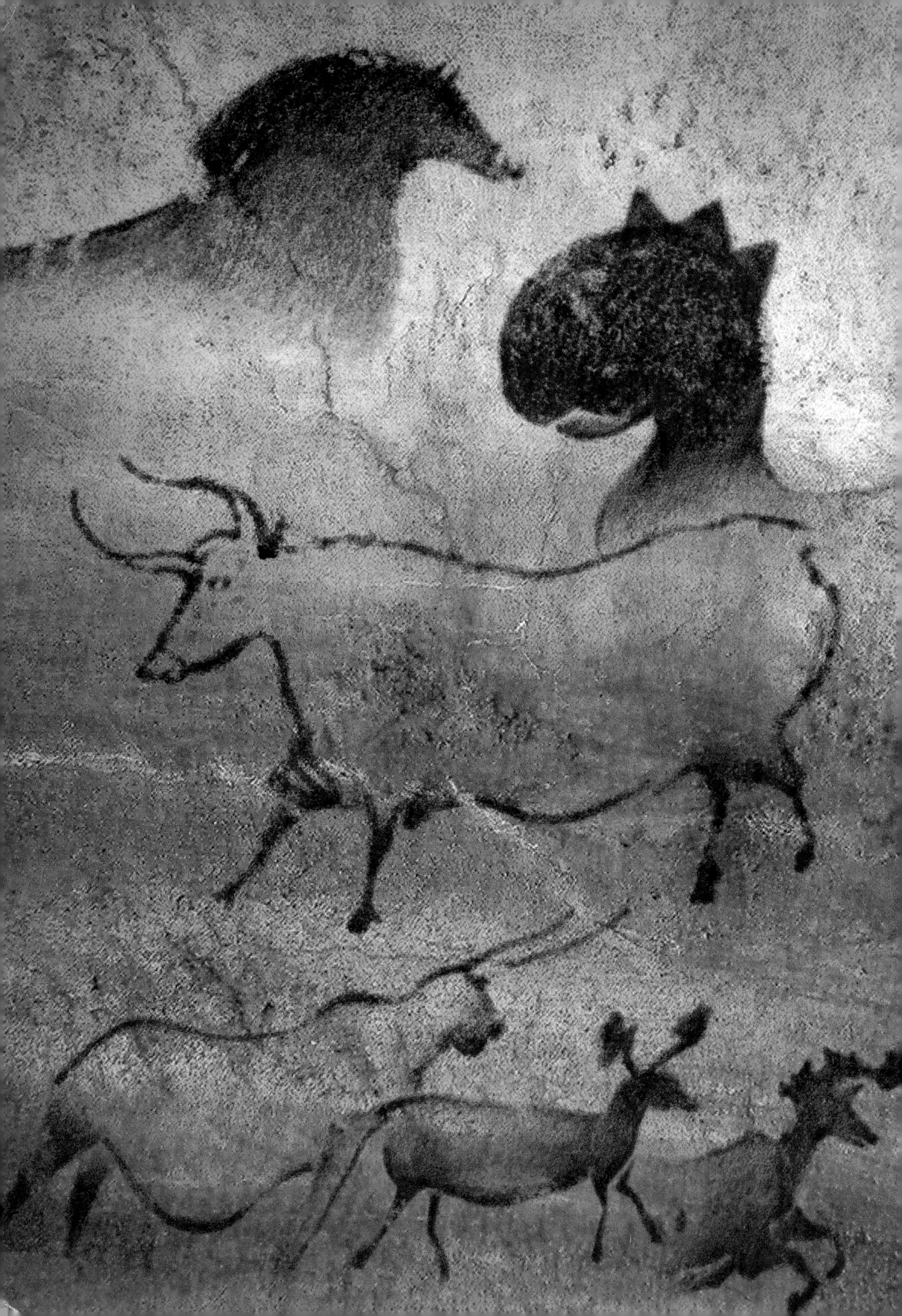

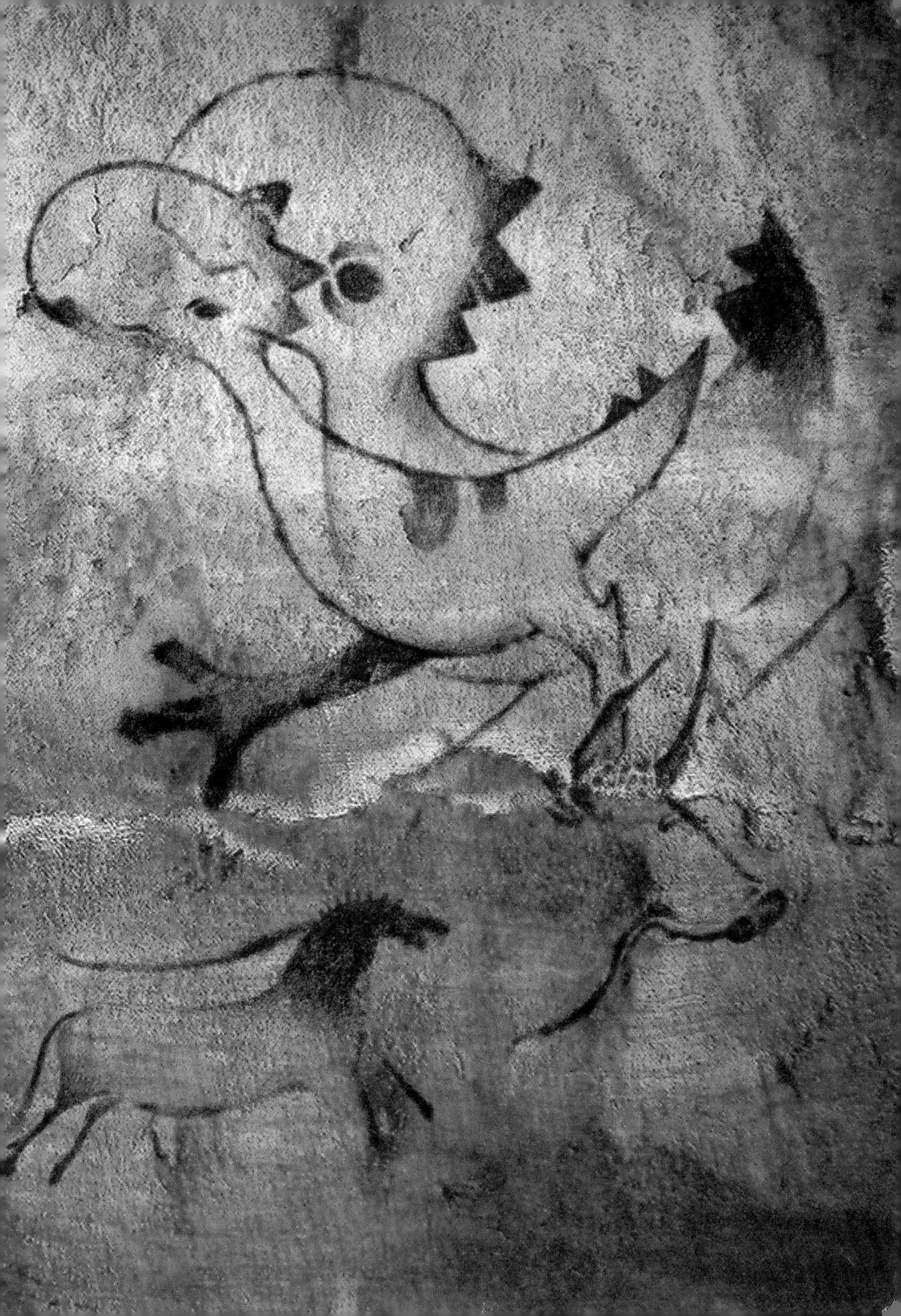